# The Unpredictability of being HUMAN

## LINNI INGEMUNDSEN

### USBORNE

The
Unpredictability
of being
HUMAN

First published in the UK in 2018 by Usborne Publishing Ltd., Usborne House,
83-85 Saffron Hill, London EC1N 8RT, England. www.usborne.com

A CIP catalogue record for this book is available from the British Library.

ISBN 9781474940634 4696/01 JFMAMJJASO D/17

Printed in the UK.

# 1

# You, Me and God Himself

If I got to be God for one day, the first thing I'd do would be to microwave a bag of popcorn to perfection. Where all the corns got popped and not a single corn burned. And then I'd make sure that everyone else who made popcorn that day had their bags cooked to perfection too. I think a lot of people would be happy that day.

The next thing I might do is to take back what happened that day in Holberg's shop, because that was pretty silly. But then again, maybe I wouldn't undo it, because if I hadn't shoplifted that day I wouldn't have met Hanna Kjerag. You might ask why I don't change things around so that I met Hanna anyway, but I don't think it works that way. I think that's cheating.

I'd like to say that I'd end world hunger and create world peace and fix everything else that's wrong in this world. But I honestly wouldn't touch any of that. I figure that if it was *that* easy, God would have taken care of it all a long time ago. Who knows what sort of trouble I'd stir up if I started messing with that on my first day on the job?

So I'd stick to simpler things, like popcorn. Popcorn can't cause too much trouble. Besides, it's the small things in life that matter. That's what my Norwegian teacher, Trude Fjell, says.

My name is Malin Sande and I am fourteen years old. Last week I was given a school assignment: *What would you do if you got to be God for one day?*

I failed.

I failed because they said I didn't take the task seriously. All the kids who said that they wanted to get rid of world hunger passed.

I live in Haasund together with just about 5,346 other people. Unless you're from Haasund or any of the neighbouring villages, you won't have heard about the place.

Haasund is a village on the south-western coast of Norway. To get to my house you go up Haugen Hill, which is right next to Hopstad Butcher's. Then you just continue straight ahead until you reach Thorstein Street. At the end of the street there is a great big red house. It has a huge yard, with grass cut to perfection and a privet hedge surrounding it. On each side of the driveway, two tall birch trees have formed an arch almost welcoming you in. It really is a magnificent house.

I live in the house next to it. The white one with the broken garage door. It should have been painted last summer and the lawn hasn't been mowed in a while. You'll see it when you see it.

My teacher gave me two days, four hours and thirty-six minutes to hand in a new paper on what I would do as God's substitute. So I was sitting in my room with a pen and a blank sheet of paper when my dad stormed in and yelled, "Why are you not taking your schoolwork seriously?" I said that I was. And then he stormed out again. Then my mom came in and asked me why I was being rude to my dad. They're a bit on edge these days.

The truth is that before I stole that chocolate bar I had never really been in any trouble. I've always handed in my homework on time; I've never cut class, or smoked a cigarette or anything. It's not so much because I'm such a good person. It's because I'm too much of a coward to do any of those things. I worry too much about consequences. My older brother Sigve gets in trouble all the time. He cuts class and smokes cigarettes and stays out past his curfew.

7

And he doesn't care one bit about consequences. Whenever he misbehaves, my dad yells and shouts and even punches the wall and throws things across the room. And then he yells some more.

It was a Wednesday afternoon, the day I got in trouble, and I was walking home from school. All of a sudden these girls, Frida Berg and Julie Losvik, came up behind me and asked me to wait up. They are the most popular girls in my class. They never talk to me. Frida and Julie don't carry their books in a backpack like I do, they have them in handbags. Proper handbags, like the ones my mom has. Only my mom's bags are a lot cheaper. The girls were both wearing puffer jackets and Sorel boots that day and they both had their hair up in French braids. Luckily one is blonde and the other a brunette, or I might not have been able to tell them apart.

"What are you up to today?" Frida said.

"Not much," I said.

Before I knew it I had walked with them over to Holberg's shop. Frida said, "You can come to my slumber party on Saturday if you want."

"Really?" I had never been to a slumber party before.

"Yes. But you have to steal something in the shop first. To show that being a part of our group really matters to you. All the other girls have done it."

"What do I have to steal?"

"Anything."

Frida and Julie waited outside while I went into the shop. I didn't really want to steal, but these girls had never shown any interest in me before and now I had the chance to become their friend. Besides, I didn't want them to think that I was a coward.

I walked up to a shelf and grabbed the first thing I saw. A Stratos chocolate bar. I don't even like Stratos.

I put it behind my back really quickly. Then I got nervous because I realized that I had forgotten to check if anyone was watching me. I started walking backwards towards the door and I didn't see where I was going so I bumped into this girl. Our collision made me drop the chocolate and it also caused a bag of gummy bears to fall out from underneath her jacket. Apparently she was on the same mission as me. Through the window I could see that Frida and Julie were already fleeing down Valen Street. And then Holberg himself came over to us with this really strict look on his face and said, "You girls better come with me."

"You idiot!" the girl hissed at me. The girl was Hanna Kjerag.

We were sitting in the office in the back of the shop while Holberg called our parents. Hanna was wearing dark eye make-up and had a grey beanie hat on her head. She seemed to be mad at the world.

She asked me why I was trying to shoplift when I was so bad at it. I told her what had happened. Hanna raised one eyebrow and said, "You've got worse problems than I thought."

She said I needed better friends. Maybe that's why she decided to become my friend. Hanna taught me that a friend worth having is someone who doesn't make you do anything you don't want to do. She is only a year above me, but she has already had her sixteenth birthday. Perhaps that is why she knows all these things.

Hanna told me not to worry so much and to listen to my heart. My heart told me that I wanted to try and smoke a cigarette.

If I got to be God for one day I'd make sure that everyone had a friend like Hanna. And I wouldn't change a thing about that day in Holberg's shop.

Well, perhaps I'd steal a bag of popcorn instead of the Stratos bar. I hate Stratos.

I still wouldn't fix world peace and end world hunger. If God Himself can't fix it, how could I?

## 2

# Lunch

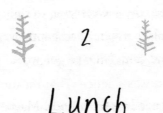

The next day the bell rang for lunch break at 11.03. It's supposed to ring at 11.00. The bells in my school are never on time. As soon as we walked out of the classroom, all the other kids gathered together in their regular groups. The girls who carry their books in handbags are in one group. The boys who like football are in another. I don't have a group.

I usually spend my lunch breaks reading. After I've eaten.

My mom used to pack my lunch for me. She would mostly make me a sandwich with ham and cheese or salami. Sometimes she would also put a piece of fruit or some biscuits in my lunch box. But around six months ago she began forgetting stuff like that more and more. When my mom started changing, my dad started yelling. Not at her though. At me. Or Sigve, or anyone else, really. Whenever my mom forgot to make my lunch, I would go hungry. So I started making it myself.

My next class was science. That meant that we would be in the chemistry lab instead of our regular classroom. I decided to go and sit down outside the lab until class started. That way I could read all the way up until the bell rang. I quickly checked the time on my OTS watch. It showed 11.07.

I have had my watch for ages. It is white and blue and has an analogue and a digital display. It is set by the world clock and automatically changes for summer and wintertime. It is also supposed to change by itself if I go to another time zone, but I have never been outside Scandinavia so I can't know for sure.

The cheese in my sandwich was all sweaty, except for the edges, which were hard and crispy. The sandwiches that my mom used to make were a lot better. I don't know how she managed to keep the cheese fresh.

After I finished my sandwich I took the book I am currently reading out of my bag. A one-volume encyclopedia. I checked it out of the library last week and it has a lot of interesting facts in it. People don't really use encyclopedias any more, so it is an older one and a bit outdated, but I still like to read it. I opened it up at a random place like I always do.

## Black panther:

Refers to wild cats that have a black coat due to melanism (opposite of albinism). The term "black panther" refers to black cats in three different species: jaguar, leopard and puma.

This information wasn't entirely correct. Melanistic pumas have never been documented and there is no proof they actually exist.

Before I had the chance to read anything else, I heard a voice.

"Let's go."

I looked up from my book and met Hanna's eyes.

"Where are we going?" I said.

She shrugged. "Does it matter?" And then she started walking down the hallway.

I collected my things and hurried after her.

We went to the toilets behind the gym where a lot of kids go to smoke. It always smells like wet metal in there. Hanna put a cigarette in her mouth and lit it up. She took a long drag and blew the smoke at the mirror. She caught me looking at her and raised one eyebrow. "Do you want one?"

I put the cigarette in my mouth and Hanna lit it for me. I sucked on it and held the smoke in my mouth for a bit before blowing it out.

Hanna said, "You have to inhale when the smoke is in your mouth. Drag it down to your lungs. Or else there is no point."

I tried. I coughed. I did it a couple more times. It made me feel dizzy and nauseous.

"You don't have to smoke the whole thing," Hanna said. She took the cigarette from me and gently put it out on the sink, before putting it back in the box.

"What did your parents say?" I asked.

"About what?"

"The Holberg's thing."

Hanna shrugged. "The usual. Yours?"

"My dad yelled."

"And?"

"That's it."

After I said goodbye to Hanna I walked over to the chemistry lab. It was still five minutes and forty-one seconds until the break was over. As I was about to walk into the room, a voice said, "Malin."

I turned around to see who it was. It was Frida. She was with Julie.

"How's it going?" Frida said.

"Fine," I said.

"Sorry about the thing at Holberg's shop the other day," Frida said. "We were just joking, we didn't think you would actually go through with it."

"Yeah, totally," Julie agreed.

I didn't say anything.

"So, anyway," Frida continued, "I would love to invite you to that slumber party, but unfortunately it got cancelled."

I looked past her and into the classroom, where some kids were already finding their seats. I still felt sick from the cigarette.

"But I've got something else in store that I think you'll be just as excited about." She looked at me as if she was waiting for me to say something. "Don't you want to know what it is?"

"Sure," I said.

"I am arranging a school prom. It will be great. We will wear fancy dresses and have streamers hanging from the ceiling and black and silver balloons."

"Just like the proms in all the American TV series," Julie said.

"Okay," I said. Because I didn't know what else to say.

"The problem is", Frida said, "that we spoke to Principal

Skogen and he told us there is no budget for a school prom because of that trip to the museum."

She was talking about a trip to Stavanger Museum. We were going to see an exhibition called *Time*, where they were displaying a lot of different clocks from different times in history. They also had a workshop where you could make your own cuckoo clock. I had been looking forward to going for weeks.

"So anyway," Frida said, pulling a sheet out from her bag, "I have made this petition saying that we would rather have a prom than go to the museum." Frida tucked her perfect brown hair behind her ear and tilted her head. "I mean I think it is pretty clear that everyone would."

"Yeah, totally." Julie nodded. "And if everyone signs it, they will have no choice but to let us have the prom instead."

Frida held the sheet out to me. "So will you sign it?"

"No," I said.

Then the bell rang.

In our next break, Frida came up to me again and said that I was being really selfish because everyone else was signing the petition. So if the prom didn't happen it would be all my fault and everyone would be really mad at me. I didn't say anything because I had to think. I don't like people being mad at me, but I really wanted to try and make a clock.

Then Frida said, "I can get you nominated for prom queen. Me and Julie are the ones in charge, so we make all the decisions."

"I don't want to be prom queen."

"Don't you want to be popular? Everyone who's nominated for prom queen becomes popular."

Being popular did sound nice. Once someone let the air out of my bike tyres and I had to walk my bike all the way home. That probably wouldn't have happened if I was popular.

Frida smiled and handed me a pen and I rolled it back and forth in my hand for a bit. And then, just as I was about to sign my name, someone yanked the pen out of my hand. I looked up.

Hanna was back.

"She said no," Hanna said.

Frida took a quick look at Julie before saying, "I think she can decide that for herself, don't you?"

"She just did. She said no."

"And who are you?" Frida asked.

"I'm her friend."

No one had ever called me their friend before.

* * *

Later, Hanna said, "Why were you talking to Frida anyway?"

I shrugged. "She was the one talking to me."

"She is not your friend." Hanna raised one eyebrow and looked at me. "She will never be your friend."

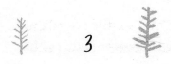

# 3

# A Shoulder to Cry On

A couple of days later my brother Sigve shot seventy-nine people. Some in the head. Some in the chest. A few in the back. All of them were soldiers fighting for the other side.

He doesn't like to shoot them in the back, he says. He likes it better when they see it coming.

He really enjoys these video games of his.

My dad ran down to the basement and told Sigve that he couldn't stay inside his entire Sunday. He told him to turn off the Xbox and go outside. He shouted, "Get some fresh air! Go meet your friends!"

Sigve said that he wouldn't.

Then I told my dad that I was going out to meet my friend Hanna.

My dad said, "Are you talking about the girl you met in Holberg's shop?"

"Yes."

"You can't be friends with that girl!"

"Why not?"

"She was stealing!"

"So was I."

Then he stormed upstairs, shouting that I was impossible to reason with.

When my dad took a nap, I biked down to Naerheim Woods to meet Hanna. I found her smoking by the large oak tree, where the benches are. When she saw me she offered me a cigarette. That's her way of saying hello. "No thanks," I said. "I'm all right."

Smoking a cigarette wasn't as exotic as I had imagined.

Hanna said that she had to choose her elective courses by the next day.

"What are you going to choose?" I asked.

Hanna shrugged. "Who cares?"

She finished her cigarette while I unsuccessfully tried to comb my hair with my fingers. My hair seems to have a life of its own. Sigve wakes up in the morning with his hair all over the place but it still looks all right. Like he made an effort to get it to look like that. Me, I comb my hair for an hour and it still looks like it got caught in a hedge cutter. I wonder who I got these brown curls from?

"Maybe you got them from your dad," Hanna suggested.

"My dad doesn't have curly hair."

Hanna raised one eyebrow. "Maybe he does."

"What do you mean?"

"Maybe your dad isn't your dad."

I decided that my hair was as good as it could get and stopped messing with it.

Hanna suggested that we should bike down to Holberg's shop. And this time we had money. Holberg was pretty okay about the whole thing. He'd agreed not to press charges because he knows my parents. He knows Hanna's parents too. Holberg knows everybody.

As we biked down Njaal Street I saw these two boys from my class, Kjetil Holmvik and Gjermund Moen. They were smoking by the pine trees a little off the road. Kjetil was laughing at something, so I could see his new braces. It's funny, whenever you see someone with braces holding a cigarette, you know they're too young to smoke. Or too old to have braces. Gjermund doesn't have braces. He doesn't need them. His teeth are perfect.

I guess I forgot to look where I was going. The truth is that I always have been a bit clumsy. So I ran my bike right into this big branch that was lying in the middle of the road.

I flew over the handlebars, dived towards the asphalt and landed on my right shoulder. I heard something pop. I waited for a couple of seconds before trying to get up, because I knew straight away that something wasn't right. And then, when I tried to move my arm, it hurt really badly. In fact, any movement made my arm hurt.

"Malin? Are you okay?" Hanna said.

"My arm doesn't work."

Hanna tried to call my parents but neither of them answered their phone. We weren't too far away from the middle of Haasund, so she asked me if I would be all right to walk down to the medical centre.

"No," I said.

Then I did it anyway.

Hanna walked ahead with our bikes. I walked behind with my left arm supporting my right arm. The wind kept blowing my hair in my face and I had no free hand to remove it with. Stupid curls. Even though I was supporting my arm, it still hurt to walk. With every step I took, pain shot through me.

It took us about twenty minutes to walk from Njaal Street to the medical centre on Berg Street. It normally takes five minutes. When we walked into the emergency department, there were a lot of people in the waiting room. Young people bleeding. Old people coughing.

I stopped this nurse walking by and said, "I need help. I don't know what's wrong with me."

The nurse didn't even need to examine me. She just glanced at me and said, "You have dislocated your shoulder."

The woman behind the counter put all my information into the computer. My name, my address and my parents' phone numbers.

She asked me if I had any ID.

I didn't.

She asked me if I knew my social security number.

I didn't.

She said that they would call my mom and dad, and they couldn't do anything to help me before at least one of my parents was present.

Sit down and wait, she said. Have a cup of water, she said.

I had no free hand to hold the cup with. Hanna helped me get a drink of water before I took a seat.

Then I started crying. Sometimes when you don't know what to do with yourself all you can do is cry. I cried so much that I started sobbing. But the sobbing caused more pain in my arm. Every tiny little movement hurt. So I stopped crying.

"It's going to be okay," Hanna said.

I wondered if my mom had forgotten that she was supposed to come to the emergency room. She has forgotten a lot of things lately.

One hour, forty-three minutes and twenty-seven seconds later, my mom finally rushed in. She was shouting at the staff and waving her arms with panic in her eyes. I wondered how she would react in a real emergency. My mom gave Hanna a lollipop and told her that she would take over now. She doesn't realize how embarrassing she is.

The nurse showed us into the examination room and said that she would give me something for the pain. I sat down on a chair and she put a needle in a vein on my left hand.

She gave me a dose of something called morphine. I felt the medicine run through my blood, and the pain eased up instantly. I'd take this over a cigarette any day. Then the doctor came in and told me to take my shirt off.

"I can't," I said. "I can't move my arm."

"You have to do it anyway," he said.

I didn't do anything. I just looked at him.

The doctor turned to my mom. She was standing in the corner, holding her handbag in a tight grip. I think he was waiting for her to say something, but she didn't. She doesn't really get involved much these days.

24

The doctor looked at me again. "Okay," he said.

Then he got me to lie face down on a bed with my detached arm dangling at the side. Next he put a bucket of water on the floor and told me to grab hold of the handle. And then he started to increase the height of the bed. "Stretching your arm out should make your shoulder slip back into position," he said. I waited for a pop that never came. But then suddenly the doctor said, "I think we've got it!"

*No way*, I thought. But then I tried to move it and he was right. My arm worked again! The nurse put a sling around my arm and told me to keep it on for a week. "If it ever happens again you could try this at home," she said. Then she walked away. And then the doctor came over and told me never to try this at home.


Afterwards, I got to choose dinner. Anything I wanted. I chose Grandiosa frozen pizza and ate it in front of the TV. My mom told me that I could stay home from school the next day.

At 9.36 p.m. I was lying in bed thinking about the comment Hanna made about my dad and my curly hair. And so I played with the thought of my dad not being my dad. That somewhere out there, there was a man with brown curly hair who was my real father. A man who would hug me goodnight, and ask me how my day was. And care.

As I was thinking about my perfect dad, my actual dad walked into my room. The one with the straight hair and the moustache.

He said, "How's the arm?"

"It's all right."

"I told you not to hang out with that girl."

"It wasn't her fault."

He didn't say anything so I said, "I'm seeing her again tomorrow."

"No you're not. Stay inside. Take it easy. Play some video games."

As he walked out of my room he tripped over some dirty laundry on the floor and barged into the wall. I heard him cursing as he walked into the living room.

And I thought: *That guy is definitely my dad. No doubt about it.*

# 4

# Domestic Silence

My dad told me to go down to the basement and shoot some people in the head so I did. But it was hard to hold the controller with my arm in the sling, so I turned off the Xbox after a few minutes. You never really know how much you need both arms until you have just one.

Sigve doesn't like it when I touch his Xbox, so I tried to leave everything just the way I found it. The Xbox was exactly eleven centimetres from the back wall and it was rotated thirty-seven degrees to the left. And the controller was on top. Before I was born, Sigve had three whole years as an only child. Maybe he liked it that way. Maybe that is why he hates me.

My mom said I had to take a day off and rest. It was

weird being in the house when everything was so quiet. My mom was answering phone calls at her office. My dad was making phone calls at *his* office. Sigve was at school. Quiet.

At 11.04 a.m. I went into the kitchen to get myself a glass of chocolate milk. As I walked through the living room I thought I saw a shadow passing by the window. By the time I turned around it was gone. And then, a couple of seconds later, I could feel someone staring at me through the sliding door that leads to the terrace. I slowly turned around and found myself looking straight into the eyes of someone I knew well. It was Oscar. He didn't say anything. He didn't move. He just stared at me with his yellowish eyes, as if waiting for me to do something. And so I opened the door to let him in.

Oscar is my cat. He is black and fluffy and when I opened the door he ran in with his raggedy tail straight up in the air. Then he started rubbing his body against my legs while purring and meowing. He does that a lot these days to let us know he wants food. Oscar is on a strict diet because the vet said that he was too fat. He's only allowed to eat fifty-five grams of dry cat food per day. But I figure Oscar wouldn't be meowing so often if he wasn't hungry, so I sneak him treats when no one is watching me. Which is more often than you'd think.

I opened a can of tuna for Oscar and poured myself a glass of chocolate milk. Then I went into the living room and turned on the TV. I didn't want to watch anything, I just wanted some noise. When you're used to yelling, silence is scary.

I rarely get the house to myself so I felt that I should make the most of it. I decided to sneak around and go through secret drawers and cupboards. Maybe I'd find papers that prove I'm adopted. Or the death certificate of my real dad. Or money.

The thing is, we don't really have any secret drawers or cupboards. So I took my glass of chocolate milk and went into my parents' room. I found a bottle of white wine in my mom's sock drawer. And a photograph of Magnus in my dad's bedside drawer. Nothing out of the ordinary.

Then I went into Sigve's room. His clothes were all over the floor, and on his desk there were four empty Coke bottles and a plate with leftover pizza on it. I snooped around there for a while, but because of all the mess I got really nervous that I wouldn't be able to put everything back exactly where I found it, so I left his room.

At 2.21 p.m. Hanna called me and told me she needed a favour. She said, "I have a date with Patrik on Saturday."

29

Patrik is her boyfriend. He is one year older than her (he turns seventeen this year) and they have been together for a really long time. Over a month.

Hanna continued, "And the thing is he is kind of stuck looking after his little brother. I mean he's thirteen and all, but he is not allowed to be home alone after he tried to burn down their garage."

"Okay?"

"Yeah, so I was wondering if you might be willing to tag along and keep his brother company. You might even know who he is? Ruben Oftedal."

I do know who Ruben Oftedal is. He is a year below me. Supposedly someone paid him twenty kroner to eat a grasshopper when he was in the second grade, so I guess he's a little bit weird. And also: he tried to burn down a garage. But last summer I saw him helping a little girl who fell off her bike, so he seems nice too. And he has the same haircut as Timothée Chalamet, which is kind of cool.

"He knows who you are anyway," Hanna said. "He thinks you're cute. So are you in?"

"Okay."

"Thanks, Malin. Hey, make sure you have fresh breath on Saturday."

"What?"

Hanna laughed. "Hey, you're going on a date. Doesn't hurt to be prepared."

"What do you mean?"

Hanna laughed. "He might want to kiss you."

Most of the girls in my class had kissed boys already and I was thinking that I should know how to do this already, but I didn't.

I went into the room that my dad calls his study, and sat down in front of the computer.

When I typed in *How to kiss...* Google came up with these suggestions:

*How to kiss a frog*
*How to kiss a girl*
*How to kiss good*
*How to kiss a boy for the first time*
*How to kiss with tongue*

Apparently there are more people out there who want to know how to kiss a frog than how to kiss a boy. That's weird. I mean, I'm pretty sure that the frog wouldn't care either way.

I clicked on the first link *How to kiss a boy for the first time*.

The article had four main points:

1. Before the kiss
2. Leaning into the kiss
3. During the kiss
4. After the kiss

Each point was explained in detail:

- Lock eyes with him and move your body closer to him to indicate that you want him to kiss you. Pucker your lips.
- Keep your eyes open as you lean into the kiss, and close them just before making lip contact. Tilt your head as you lean in to avoid bumping noses.
- Breathe in and out through your nose. For your first kiss don't linger too long. Begin to pull away after five seconds.
- Open your eyes and smile at the boy you just shared a kiss with.

I guess I didn't realize how complicated this kissing thing was until I googled it. I printed out a copy of the article so I could study it later. And then I also clicked on the link *How to kiss with tongue* just to be on the safe side. It doesn't hurt to be prepared.

\* \* \*

At 3.42 p.m. Sigve came home and went down to the basement.

At 4.36 p.m. my mom came home and got started on dinner.

At 4.42 p.m. my dad came home and went straight into his study.

At 4.46 p.m. my mom said, "Oscar is looking thinner already."

At 5.11 p.m. Sigve started yelling at me for messing up his current game of *Call of Duty*.

At 5.17 p.m. my dad started yelling at me for googling *How to kiss with tongue*.

And at 5.21 p.m. I turned the TV off, because everything was back to normal.

## 5

# Domestic Tension

I fell asleep in PE. I was sitting at the side, watching my class play dodgeball (I couldn't play because I had to have my arm in the sling for another four days and sixteen hours). I was fine with watching, because no matter what game we're playing (football, handball, field hockey, volleyball or basketball), I always seem to end up getting hit in the head with a ball.

I was really tired so I nodded off for a couple of minutes. And I woke up on the floor with my teacher, Haakon Krag, splashing water in my face because he thought that I had passed out. He smelled of garlic and Fisherman's Friend. Some of my classmates laughed at me, but most of them were just annoyed because I held up the game. I told

Haakon that I was okay, and then I went and sat on one of the exercise balls, because I figured it would be harder to fall asleep if I was sitting on a ball. Then I was so busy trying not to fall asleep that I forgot to pay attention and I got hit with the ball a couple of times. I wasn't even playing and I still got hit in the head.

I couldn't sleep last night because I was worried that I would wake up with Sigve standing over my bed holding a sharp object.

At 7.03 p.m. the day before, I was on my way to the toilet and suddenly Sigve jumped in front of me and blocked the entrance to the bathroom. He had murder in his eyes and a half-empty glass of chocolate milk in his hand. He held up the glass and said, "Forget something?"

I guessed I'd left my glass somewhere but Sigve isn't normally too concerned about dirty dishes so I didn't understand why he was so worked up. Then I realized that I must have left it in his room. I tried to think of an excuse for me to have been in his room, but it was hard to concentrate because I really had to pee.

But he didn't ask me why I had been in his room. Instead he said, "So where is it?" His voice was calm, but he sounded really mad.

"Where is what?" I said.

"You know what I mean."

But I didn't. All I found in his room were dirty clothes and leftover pizza.

Then he said, "If you don't give it back within the next few hours I will kill you in your sleep." And then he walked off.

As I didn't take anything from his room, I obviously couldn't return it, so I tried to stay awake all night. I figured he couldn't kill me in my sleep if I was awake.

My mom works part-time as a secretary down at Haasund Pipes. I knew she got off work early on Thursdays so I could go home straight after school without worrying about being alone with Sigve.

When I came home my mom had already started on dinner. She was making a venison casserole and she said it tastes better if you let it cook for a while. She stirred the pot and put some red wine in it. Then she poured some red wine in a glass and took a sip, while continuing to stir the pot. A glass of red wine is good for the heart, she says. My mom has a great heart.

At 2.35 p.m. Aunt Lillian, who is my mom's sister, and Magnus, who is my cousin, came over. They live over on Knuds Street, which is just a ten-minute walk from our house. I don't know who Magnus's dad is and I don't think Magnus does either. Magnus is sixteen and my favourite cousin. He always lets me tag along and he doesn't yell at me or tell me to shut up. I think it's because he doesn't have any siblings. He doesn't know how it feels to truly hate someone.

Magnus is a swimming champion. He's got a lot of trophies in his room and he's famous in all of Haasund. Recently he's been practising swimming underwater, and when he arrived he asked me if I could help him with something. We went into the bathroom and he filled a bucket with lukewarm water. He put the bucket on the floor and kneeled down next to it. He pointed at my watch. "Time me." Then he took a deep breath and put his head in the bucket and I turned the timer on. I watched the numbers on the display increasing: 1, 2, 3, 4, 5, 6, 7, 8…

It took for ever before Magnus came back up. I thought about Sigve and wondered if he was still mad. I thought about Ruben Oftedal and wondered what kind of music he listens to. I thought about Frida Berg and wondered how she got her hair to look so perfect all the time. Then I thought about Magnus, who had his head in a bucket on my bathroom floor, and wondered if he was okay. I said, "Are you okay?" But he didn't answer, and I started wondering if I had to go and get help.

But then he pulled his head out of the bucket. He exhaled loudly and spat out water, and tons of water dripped from his head down his red jumper and onto the bathroom floor.

I pressed stop on the timer and said, "Four minutes and forty-six seconds."

He smiled and said, "New personal record."

I showed him where we keep the towels so he could dry himself off.

"You should try and do some swimming when you get your sling off," Magnus said. "Swimming is good for your shoulder."

Afterwards, we went into the living room and watched an old episode of *Glee*.

"This show is terrible," Magnus said.

"I know," I said, "but I like it anyway."

At 4.35 p.m. my dad came home from work. He mumbled hello and took the remote and switched to the TV2 Sport channel which was showing an ice hockey match. He turned to Magnus and said, "The Oilers are doing well this year. We should go and see them sometime."

Magnus looked confused. "Okay...sure."

My dad usually doesn't offer to take anyone anywhere and Magnus is not into sports so it was really weird.

When my dad wasn't looking Magnus mouthed, "What the hell?" at me.

I shrugged and tried to hide that I was laughing.

At 5.03 p.m. dinner was ready, so me and Magnus went into the kitchen. The smell of food made Oscar circle around the table, meowing.

"That cat drives me crazy sometimes," my mom said and let him out. Then she called my dad: "Leif! Dinner is ready!"

He didn't answer so she called him again. "Leif! Dinner! I'm not going to tell you again."

And then three minutes later she called him again.

When my dad finally came in, there was a free seat between my mom and Aunt Lillian, but he asked me to switch with him because that seat was right under the lamp and the light was too bright and hurt his eyes, he said.

So I switched seats and took a spoonful of meat with gravy and mashed potatoes. I really like venison casserole but I couldn't enjoy it properly because I kept worrying that the light from the lamp would hurt my eyes.

Aunt Lillian was saying that she had been seeing this guy for a few weeks, but she didn't think it would work out.

"Why not?" My mum laughed and took a sip of her wine. "Is he married?"

My dad started coughing and Aunt Lillian said, "Can someone pass the salt, please?"

Sigve didn't come home until 8.59 p.m. He said he had

eaten and went straight down to the basement. And he didn't say anything else about me being in his room. Maybe he found whatever he thought he was missing.

# 6

# Dates and Don'ts

Dating has a lot of rules: don't talk about yourself all night; don't talk about previous relationships; don't get drunk. At least that's what the internet says. It didn't seem too hard. I knew I wasn't going to talk about myself (or anything else) all night, because we were meeting during daytime. I don't have any previous relationships and we're both too young to drink.

At 2.11 p.m. Hanna and I walked over to Patrik and Ruben's house. They live on Asp Street which is about a fifteen-minute walk from the centre of Haasund.

Hanna suggested we take our bikes, but I have my arm in a sling for one day and twenty-one minutes more, so I wanted to walk. I didn't tell my mom and dad where I was going. Mainly because they didn't ask, but also because I didn't know if they would like that I was going to see a boy. I am not too worried about getting into trouble any more though. All that happens is that my dad yells at me. Which he does anyway.

As we walked we didn't talk about the date. Instead Hanna was telling me this story about how her science teacher had it in for her, because he was always asking her questions he knew she couldn't answer.

My mind started to drift away a little. I noticed we were passing the old Odland farm. That meant that we were almost there and suddenly I felt a little nauseous.

We arrived at their house at 2.25 p.m. and Patrik showed us into the living room.

Ruben sat on a huge corner sofa. He was wearing a black hoodie that said *Vans* and a bright blue DC cap.

"Hi, Malin," he said.

"Hello," I said.

Patrik led Hanna by her hand and sat down on the other end of the sofa. Hanna sat on top of him and put her hand on the back of his neck and he stroked her thighs as they started kissing.

The internet had said, *If everything goes well, you might want to end the date with a kiss. Make eye contact – longer than you normally would – and maybe gently bite your bottom lip, to look kissable.*

This was the beginning of the date and Hanna and Patrik were kissing now. Already the internet was wrong.

I sat down next to Ruben. He pointed at my sling and said, "What happened?"

"I fell off my bike."

"Did it hurt?"

"Yes."

I looked around the room. By one of the walls there was a sideboard filled with knick-knacks – an unplugged lamp, a green vase and some pictures of people I didn't know. There was also a giant ceramic bulldog next to a tiny clown. I couldn't decide which was creepier.

Ruben said, "I heard you shoplifted at Holberg's."

"I heard you burned down a garage."

"That's not true," he said and looked at the floor. "I wasn't successful." Then he looked at me and smiled. "Brick walls are very solid."

Hanna and Patrik were breathing heavier from their corner of the sofa and Patrik moved his hand from Hanna's thigh up under her shirt. I wondered if they had forgotten that Ruben and I were in the room. On TV, this was usually the moment where couples got interrupted. By a parent or a younger sibling. Or something else. I wondered if I should interrupt them.

Suddenly Hanna and Patrik broke free from each other and Hanna said, "We're going for a walk." And then they got up from the sofa and left the room. But they didn't put their shoes and coats on. They just went into the next room.

I guess I hadn't done enough research beforehand, because there was nothing on the internet about this either. I had no idea what would happen next and my heart started beating faster and my palms were sweaty.

Then Ruben said, "Do you want to play some video games?"

And I said, "Okay," and my heart went back to beating at a normal pace.

We played a car racing game and I was trying to control a monkey wearing a sombrero, but I wasn't able to steer properly with only one hand. I kept driving my car off the track and Ruben crossed the finish line before I had even passed the first checkpoint. "I'm not very good at this," I said.

Ruben shrugged and said, "It's a pretty stupid game anyway." And then he turned the Xbox off.

If the kissing doesn't happen at the end of the date, how do you know when it starts? I closed my eyes and tried to remember what the internet had taught me:

*Keep your eyes open as you lean into the kiss, and close*

44

*them just before making lip contact. Tilt your head as you lean in to avoid bumping noses.*

But Ruben just sat quietly for a couple of minutes. And then he said, "What's your favourite colour?"

"Blue."

"Oh. Mine's red."

"Oh."

We didn't say anything for a while and I wondered if *now* was the time he was going to kiss me.

*Breathe in and out through your nose. For your first kiss don't linger too long. Begin to pull away after five seconds.*

Then Ruben said, "What's your favourite TV show?"

"*The Ranch*. And *Riverdale*. And sometimes *One Tree Hill* even though it is super old."

"Cool. I like watching *Bondi Rescue*. Someone nearly drowned on that show last week."

"My cousin, Magnus, is a really good swimmer," I said. And then I didn't say anything else, because I realized that I was talking about other boys and I didn't know if Ruben liked that. Even if I was talking about my cousin.

"Wait," Ruben suddenly said and got up and left the room.

*Wait.* That's all he said. What was I waiting for? There was nothing about this on the internet either. I looked at the ceramic clown. It was grinning at me. I'm pretty sure it hadn't been doing that earlier.

Three minutes and forty-two seconds later, Ruben came back. "Look," he said. What do people show each other on a first date? I was afraid to look, so I just kept staring at the clown. "It's from Gran Canaria," Ruben said. And so I turned and looked at him and saw that he was holding a small stone. "We were there on holiday last summer and I found it on the beach." He held out his hand. "Feel how smooth it is." I stroked the stone with my left index finger. He was right. It was very smooth. My finger accidentally touched the palm of his hand and it felt warm against my cold skin. "You can keep the stone if you want," Ruben said.

A couple of minutes later Hanna and Patrik came back. Hanna looked flushed and had her shirt on backwards, which I hadn't noticed earlier.

"Are you ready to go?" she said.

Patrik half-smiled and said, "Our parents will be home soon."


On our way back Hanna talked a lot. Something about boys and how they were hard to read sometimes. I wasn't really listening.

I thought about how my date was over and how I still hadn't kissed a boy. And that was okay. Dating isn't really like what the internet says anyway.

I put my left hand in my coat pocket and felt the smooth surface of the stone. The stone was from Gran Canaria. The stone was from Ruben Oftedal.

When I came home my dad yelled at me because I was late and I hadn't told anyone where I was going. I didn't care too much though. There is nothing new about my dad yelling.

# 7

# Don't Speak

On Monday morning my mom's eyes were glassy and her mouth was stern. She said that she had a headache and told me to leave her alone and not to make any noise. Luckily I had to go to school. I walked into my room and packed my bag as quietly as I could. Then I put my coat and shoes on and slipped out the door. I made sure to close the door properly and to do it silently.

I carried my backpack over my left shoulder, which was hard because I had a lot of books and it was heavy, so I had to take a lot of breaks. Luckily I was getting my sling off that afternoon. Actually I had had it on for a week the day before, but the medical centre is not open on Sundays. Only the emergency room. Getting a sling on can be urgent. Taking a sling off is not.

It normally takes me between twelve and fifteen minutes to walk to school, but with only one arm everything takes longer. Even walking. At the bottom of Haugen Hill I took another break and checked the time. It was 8.09 and I was halfway there.

Class starts at 8.15. I couldn't be late. You have to be on time. That's the rule. I put my bag back up on my shoulder and sped up. And I didn't take another break.

I walked into my classroom at 8.15 sharp. I found my desk and sat down. Three minutes later the bell rang.

In recess I was standing in the corridor, wondering if I should go and find Hanna. Her classroom is on the other side of the building, so I wasn't sure if I should risk going all the way there and all the way back when I didn't even know if she would be there.

Then someone said, "Hello, Malin." I didn't need to check who it was because I recognized the voice. It was Ruben.

I turned around and said, "Hello."

"How are you?"

"I am fine."

I reached into my pocket and took out the stone. "I still have it," I said.

"It is a good stone," Ruben said.

"Do you want it back?"

Ruben smiled. "No, it's yours."

I smiled too.

And then he said he had to go. "I'll talk to you later."

"Okay," I said.

I looked at the shiny grey stone. It had an oval shape, a smooth surface and was covered in tiny black dots.

Then I heard a voice right behind me that made me jump. Someone said, "Hey."

It was Frida. I didn't know how long she had been standing there.

"What were you and Ruben talking about?"

I shrugged. "Not much."

"It must have been something interesting. I can't remember seeing you smile like that before."

I stroked the stone with my thumb in a circular motion.

Then someone called Frida's name and she turned around to see who it was. Someone from her group was calling her over. Frida's group consists of her and Julie Losvik and this other girl named Norunn Setre. Sometimes they hang out with other people too, but mostly it is the three of them.

Frida looked at my hand and said, "Nice stone." And then she walked back to her friends.

\* \* \*

After school I went to the medical centre. I walked up to the counter where the lady was sitting and said, "I am here to take my sling off."

"Okay?"

"Yes," I said.

"Do you have an appointment?"

"It has been a week."

"I see."

"Yesterday."

"Excuse me?"

"It was a week yesterday."

"All right," she said.

She asked for my name and put something into the computer. Then she told me to sit down and wait.

I took a seat. There were six other people in the waiting room and they were all really old. Maybe over fifty. The walls were white and there were no pictures or anything.

And I waited.

Every now and then a lady came out and called people's names. And one by one they went in.

I waited and waited. I checked the time. It was 2.56 p.m. That meant that I had been waiting for thirty-six minutes.

People kept coming in after me, but went into the doctor's office before me.

One hour and nineteen minutes later the doctor came out to the waiting room. It was the same one who had helped me last time I was there. To the woman behind the counter he said, "I guess that is all the patients for today."

The lady pointed at me. "There is a young lady here to see you."

The doctor looked at me. "Oh," he said. "What can I help you with?"

"I have to take my sling off. It has been a week."

"Right." He looked confused. "Sorry, why are you here?"

"To take my sling off."

"Oh," he said. "Well, you can just take it off. You didn't need to come all the way down here to do that."

So I took it off. I moved my right arm around to see how it felt. It was really good to have both of my arms again.

I walked home and now I could carry my backpack normally so it was a lot easier. When I reached my house the time was 4.35 p.m. and it was already pretty dark outside. Our car was parked in the driveway so I knew that my dad had finished work.

Our neighbour, Jon Gravdal, was taking the trash out and when he saw me he said, "Hello."

"Hello."

"How are you?"

"I'm fine."

"How are your mom and dad?"

"I don't know."

"You don't know?"

"I haven't asked them."

"All right."

I looked at him.

"Well have a nice day," he said.

"Okay," I said.

I went inside the house and put down my backpack by the entrance. Then I hung up my coat on its regular hook. I took the stone out of the pocket of my coat and put it in my pencil case. That way I knew it would be safe and not fall out.

When I walked into the living room my dad was standing by the window.

"What were you talking to Gravdal about?" he said.

I shrugged. "He asked how we were doing."

"Don't be telling people our stuff."

"What stuff?"

"Any stuff. Our stuff. It is nobody's business."

"Okay." I raised my right arm. "I got my sling off," I said.

He looked at my arm. "Oh, right," he said. "Good."

I started to walk into the kitchen. In the doorway I stopped and turned around. "How are you, Dad?" I said.

"What?"

"How are you?"

"Why are you asking me that?"

I shrugged. "That is what people ask each other."

My dad looked at me. "Why don't you go and wash up for dinner?"

I went into the kitchen, where my mom was standing by the stove, cooking.

"Oh, you are home from school already," she said. "I started dinner early today, it seems. But don't worry we can eat later."

My school finishes at 2.15 p.m. I am normally home between 2.27 and 2.36 p.m. and we always have dinner sometime between 4.03 p.m. and 5.46 p.m.

"It's 4.44 p.m.," I said.

She paused. "Exactly," she said. "Well, have a seat. Dinner's almost ready."

I took my seat at the table. The smell of food was making me really hungry.

"How are you, Mom?" I said.

"I'm fantastic," my mom said.

# 8

# In Deep Water

Magnus said that swimming would help improve my shoulder muscles without putting too much strain on the joint. So I went to the pool. We only have one in Haasund and it is the one at my school. On Wednesday afternoons it is open to the public.

When I got into the locker room there were only a couple of ladies there, who looked like they were around my mom's age. They were already on their way to the showers.

Before you go into the pool you have to take a shower. Nude. And you need to use soap. It's pretty perverted. I know a lot of people don't bother, but those are the rules. I took off my clothes and folded them neatly and put them on one of the benches. The locker room doesn't actually have any lockers. Lastly I took off my OTS watch and put it on top of my clothes. I don't like taking my watch off because I like to always have the option to check what time it is.

I wrapped a towel around me and went to the showers. There was no one there. I guessed the ladies were already in the pool. I put my towel on the hook next to the shower, went in and pressed the button. I quickly soaped up and rinsed myself off. I put my swimming costume on and then I held my swimming cap under the shower so it would be easier to put on. Everyone needs to wear a swimming cap in the pool. Another rule. I pushed the cap down over my head, and tucked in all the curls that were sticking out.

As I didn't have my watch on I don't know how long the shower took me exactly. But I would guess around four and a half minutes. Then I walked upstairs to the pool area.

There were actually quite a few people swimming that day.

The pool had been split into a fast lane and a slow lane. They also had a section at the shallow end of the pool, named the Fun Pool, where a couple of younger kids were playing.

I went over to the section labelled *Slow lane* and got into the water.

But I wasn't fast enough for the slow lane. So one of the lifeguards came up to me and suggested that I might want to try my luck in the Fun Pool. No way was I going to splash around with a bunch of little kids. So I decided to never come back to the pool.

Magnus is the best swimmer in our town. He dives from the ten-metre diving tower, and he can hold his breath underwater for four minutes and forty-six seconds. And he is really fast. Magnus said that he could help me become a better swimmer. But before we got into the water, I needed more knowledge. Knowledge is power, he said. Magnus watches a lot of TV.

My first lesson was in the kitchen in Magnus's house. He put on his mom's reading glasses and asked me, "What do you do when you want to overtake someone in the pool?"

I said I'd never needed to overtake anyone in the pool.

He got annoyed. Magnus told me that to learn how to swim underwater I had to practise holding my breath above water first. I said I didn't care about swimming underwater. I just wanted to swim faster.

He called me a lousy student. I called him a lousy teacher.

That's when our lessons stopped.

Who cares about swimming anyway?

But then, a couple of days later, Magnus called me and asked me if I wanted to go to the pool in Stavanger with him. It was a little weird that he offered to help me after I called him a lousy teacher. I guess his mom must have made him. Magnus said that the pool in Stavanger had these general swimming sessions every day from 4 p.m. to 5 p.m. and he could teach me some tricks.

I really wanted to go, but I was on my period so it wasn't the best time for the pool. I know there are tampons, but I wasn't sure I could trust them. I was thinking that I should try using one in the bathtub first. Too bad we don't have a bathtub.

I told Magnus that I didn't want to go to the pool with such a lousy teacher and hung up on him. I knew that would make him need a few days to cool off. And by the time he had cooled off, I was done with my period.

I liked the pool in Stavanger a lot better than the one in Haasund. It was a lot bigger and looked a lot newer. I liked the lifeguard a lot better too. He wasn't really old like the one in Haasund and he had wavy blond hair and he smiled at me when I walked in. The pool in Stavanger also had a giant clock hanging on the wall, so I could check the time if I wanted to. I liked that but I still wished that I had a waterproof watch, because then I would never have to take it off.

Magnus told me that a good breaststroke starts under the water. He said that if I wanted to swim fast, I couldn't keep swimming with my head above the surface like a Labrador.

Then Magnus started talking a lot. Something about breathing and moving your arms in a circular motion and pushing forward. And something about huge strokes and kicking your legs. I looked at the lifeguard. He was sitting in his chair with his yellow T-shirt and red shorts. I wondered if he had a girlfriend. He probably did.

Magnus offered to hold my hand while I practised kicking my legs. Just then the lifeguard turned around and looked in our direction.

I said, "I can do it myself! You don't have to help me!" And then I swam out to the deep end of the pool. I tried to focus and remember what Magnus had said. *Huge strokes. Move your arms in circular motions. Kick your legs.* What did he say about breathing? Then I noticed the lifeguard looking in my direction again and I tried to be cool and not look like a Labrador.

Suddenly I became very aware that I was in the deep end of the pool. Nothing to hold on to. Not able to reach the bottom.

In the next moments I inhaled a lot of water. I waved my arms frantically. I tried not to breathe in, but for some reason I kept doing it. And I kept swallowing water. The last thing I remember was Magnus swimming towards me faster than I've ever seen him swim before. Then I passed out.

When I woke up, the giant clock on the wall showed the time was 4.41. I was lying on the side of the pool and I couldn't remember how I'd got there. No one was in the water any more, everyone was just standing around, watching us. Watching me. Magnus and the lifeguard leaned over me as I coughed up water from the bottom of the pool.

My nose hurt. My throat hurt. My chest ached. I wondered if they'd had to perform mouth-to-mouth on me. If so, was it performed by the guy with the wavy blond hair?

Or by my cousin?

Magnus looked at me with fear in his eyes and said, "Are you okay?"

I coughed and said in a surprisingly hoarse voice, "You nearly killed me!"

I tried not to cough again because my chest hurt too much.

The lifeguard asked me some questions to make sure

I was okay, and I was. Then me and Magnus each went to our locker rooms. I didn't even shower. I just dried off and got dressed.

I met Magnus outside and he said, "Don't tell my mom I almost killed you."

I said, "Don't tell my mom I almost died."

As we were about to leave someone yelled, "Hey! Hey you, wait up." I turned around and saw that the lifeguard was walking towards us. I wondered what he wanted. Maybe he was going to tell me that he was glad I was okay. And maybe he hoped I would come back soon. He looked at me with clear blue eyes, searching for the right words.

Then he put his hand on my shoulder and said, "Next time, you might want to try your luck in the Fun Pool."

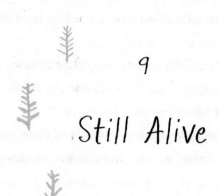

# 9

# Still Alive

We don't get much snow here in Haasund during wintertime. Mostly we just get a lot of rain. And frost. So I was excited when it started snowing the other day. I watched it from my bedroom window. It came down slow and gentle and covered Thorstein Street like a white blanket. I hoped that it would stay for a while, but I knew that it wouldn't, because Sigve had already told me that it would melt the next day and he's always right about everything.

At 2.47 p.m., Magnus came over. He was carrying his Converse messenger bag, so I guessed he'd come straight from class. I showed him into the living room but he didn't sit down. He just went around the room picking things up and looking at them for a little while, before putting them back in place. He acted like it was the first time he had been to our house.

"How's it going?" he said as he picked up one of my mom's porcelain birds from the shelf above the TV.

"Fine," I said.

He fiddled with the bird in his hand and I was nervous that he would break it. My mom loves her porcelain figurines.

"Will you stop messing with that?" I took the bird from his hand and put it back between the giraffe and the polar bear.

"Hey, thanks for not dying the other day," Magnus said.

"Don't mention it."

Magnus laughed. "Seriously though, I am glad you are okay." He shrugged. "You're like a little sister to me, you know."

I just smiled, because I'm really glad Magnus isn't my brother. If he was, he would hate me.

"Hey, check this out." Magnus took out his phone and showed me a photo of a really old-looking orange moped.

"It's a Vespa Bravo. An original one from 1982. Isn't it cool?"

It looked like a piece of junk.

I shrugged. "I guess."

"My mom said I could have it. As an early birthday present."

"But you already have a bike."

"But I want another one."

Then Sigve came in. He said a quick hello to Magnus before turning to me. "I know that you know," he said. "When are you going to tell Mom and Dad?"

As usual, I had no idea what he was talking about. So I kept my mouth shut, hoping the mystery would be revealed if I just let him keep talking.

"If you are planning on telling them, why don't you just do it? What do you want? Money?"

I kept staring at him. His icy blue eyes were locked on mine. He didn't blink. Neither did I. Then Sigve reached into the back pocket of his jeans and took out his wallet. He fished out a hundred-kroner note and held it out to me.

"This is it. I am not giving you any more. Take it or leave it."

I didn't know what I was leaving, so I took it. Then Sigve said a quick "See you later" to Magnus, before going back down to the basement.

"What was that about?" Magnus asked.

"I couldn't tell you."

"Secret?"

I nodded. It was so secret that I didn't even know myself.

"What is he up to these days anyway?" Magnus wanted to know. "I hardly ever see him any more. I haven't even seen him around school or on the train in weeks."

Magnus and Sigve both attend upper secondary school in Bryne, which is the closest city, and they have to take the train to get there. They are not in the same class though, because they are doing different courses.

I shrugged. "I don't know." Like anyone tells me anything.

Magnus stuck around for a while, and we watched TV and drank blueberry squash. My cat Oscar was playing with some dead flies on the window sill. "That's the only type of fly that cat will ever catch," Magnus said. "Man, he's fat!"

At 3.29 p.m. Magnus got up from his chair and said, "I better get going." Before leaving the room he turned and did a two-finger salute, like a scout or something. "Catch ya later." He can be really corny sometimes.

Shortly after he left, the doorbell rang. I sighed to myself as I got up to open the door. What did Magnus forget this time?

But when I opened the door it wasn't Magnus who stood on my doorstep.

It was Ruben.

"Hello, Malin," he said.

"Hello," I said.

Ruben didn't say anything else; he just stood with his hands in his pockets and looked at his shoes while he kicked a little stone around.

"Do you want to come in?" I said.

Ruben looked at me and smiled, revealing his crooked front tooth.

"Okay," he said.

We went into the living room and Ruben took a quick look around. He walked over to the side table and picked up a candlestick. He weighed it in his hand a little before putting it back.

What is up with people and their need to pick stuff up and put it down?

Ruben moved over to the shelf where my mom keeps her porcelain figurines and picked up the giraffe.

"You've got your sling off," he said.

"Yes," I said.

"That must be nice."

"Yes."

Ruben turned the giraffe upside down like he was in a shop, checking its price or something.

"Hey, Malin, I wanted to ask you something."

"Okay."

Ruben was turning the giraffe around and around. It looked like it was performing somersaults in Ruben's hands.

"I'm just curious, you know. You don't have to answer if you don't want to…"

But he didn't get to finish his sentence, because suddenly the giraffe slipped out of Ruben's hands. It plunged to the floor, and hit the parquet with a thud. The neck broke in half as soon as it hit the floor.

Ruben looked at me. "Oh my God, I'm so sorry."

"It's okay, it wasn't really important or anything."

"Maybe we could glue it back together?"

We went into the kitchen and I got the tube of glue from the big drawer with all the junk. Then we sat down at the table and I put a little glue on each piece of the giraffe. It was a pretty clean break so it was easy to stick the two pieces together, but when I let go, the top part started to slide off the bottom part so I had to grab hold of it. "Guess I have to wait until the glue dries before letting go," I said as I held the two pieces together.

"Maybe it needs more pressure," Ruben said and gently put two of his fingers on top of mine. His skin was warm and my hands started to tremble a little and I was worried that we would drop the giraffe again.

"Try now," Ruben said after a couple of seconds and

removed his fingers. I let go of the giraffe and the pieces seemed to stay together.

"I think I will leave it on the table until I'm sure that the glue is completely dry," I said. "Do you want a glass of blueberry squash?" My mom always offers drinks to her guests.

"Okay," Ruben said.

I poured two glasses of squash and then we drank it while watching the glue dry. The giraffe didn't look half bad, but I noticed that I had used a little too much glue. It lay around its neck like a transparent life preserver. Maybe it wouldn't be noticeable from a distance?

"Is there any more squash?" Ruben said.

After we finished our drinks, I put the giraffe back on the shelf. I pushed it a little further to the back and moved some of the other figurines in front, hoping the giraffe would be less noticeable. Then we watched a couple of episodes of *The Ranch*, and we both laughed in the same places. At 4.48 p.m. my dad came home and wondered who the hell had finished all the blueberry squash.

Ruben looked a little nervous and said, "I think I better go."

I said he didn't have to, and explained that my dad yelling is no big deal at all, really. But Ruben wanted to go anyway so I showed him to the door.

As he was about to leave he suddenly paused for a minute. "Malin," he said. "The thing that I wanted to ask you earlier…"

"Yes?"

"Why did you shoplift at Holberg's? I mean, you seem nice. Not like some of the other girls in your class. So I was just wondering… Why did you do it?"

"Frida Berg tricked me into it," I said. "She can be a bit mean sometimes."

"A bit mean?" Ruben laughed. "She is the Devil."

## 10

## The Devil

The Devil's plan to collect signatures failed. Not because I refused to sign the petition, but because Principal Skogen said that the trip to the museum had already been paid for. He said that the only way we could have a prom was if the students paid for it themselves. So the Devil and her sidekick started a fundraising campaign to earn money.

At recess I saw her standing with her legs crossed, holding a jar full of change, talking to a boy. The boy was Ruben Oftedal. He had his cap down over his eyes and his hands in his pocket and he was smiling while he was saying something I couldn't hear. Why was Ruben talking to the Devil?

Frida threw her head back, laughing. I am sure she laughed for several seconds, but I forgot to keep track. What could he have said that was so funny? Frida touched his shoulder and said something back, and he smiled. It felt like a tiny person was punching my stomach from the inside.

Then Ruben raised his hand to say goodbye and walked over to his friends, who were sitting at the skating ramp. Frida waved back to him. Then she caught my eye, and started walking towards me. Frida never used to talk to me at all. Lately, she had been approaching me a lot. Wanting something. As she came closer I could see that the jar was labelled *Prom*.

"Do you want to support our campaign?" She smiled her usual smile, while tilting her head slightly to the side. "You should if you want to be nominated for prom queen."

I didn't say anything. I had to think.

"Ruben already contributed."

Why would Ruben do that? Maybe he liked her now? Most boys liked Frida.

"If I were you, I would make a contribution." She looked over at the skate ramp. "Boys like prom queens, you know."

I thought about this. "So if I give you money I will be nominated?"

Frida shrugged. "Maybe. The more you contribute, the bigger the chance of getting nominated."

I looked over at Ruben, who now was having a play fight with one of his friends. His green eyes were still hidden under his cap as he struggled to keep his friend from pushing him off the ramp.

"But, hey it's up to you," Frida said and turned to walk away.

"Wait," I said.

I watched Ruben push his friend back. Even though he was smiling, he was too far away for me to see his crooked tooth. Then I gave Frida the hundred-kroner note that Sigve had given me to keep a secret I didn't even know.

Frida smiled and said, "You are way prettier than all the other girls in our class so you'll probably win the title too."

It's weird talking to Frida. She smiles and sounds friendly, but something doesn't feel right. Like if someone were to give you a compliment while kicking you in the leg. I guess that's what talking to the Devil feels like.

The morning after, just before school started, I met Hanna in the toilets behind the gym. I told her what had happened.

"You did not give that witch money?" Hanna looked at me with disbelief. Her eyes looked sore, like she hadn't got enough sleep.

"She said she could get me nominated for prom queen," I said.

Hanna raised one eyebrow and said, "Malin…"

"Yes?"

"That will never happen."

She was about to say something else, but then her face suddenly turned really white and she ran into one of the cubicles. I heard her throwing up three times before the toilet flushed and she came back out. She went over to the sink and looked at herself in the mirror, while smoothing her maroon hair. She still looked really pale. I asked her why she didn't go home if she was sick.

"I'm fine," she said and bent down to the sink to splash some water on her face.

"But I heard you," I said, "you were being sick."

Her red eyes met mine in the mirror. "Malin," she said.

"Yes," I said.

"I am not sick."

Her voice was determined so I decided not to argue. Hanna took out a packet of cigarettes from the pocket of her leather jacket. She took one cigarette out and fiddled with it between two fingers. "You know, Malin," she said, "you have to stand up to Frida at some point. If you don't she will just continue to be mean to you. And I won't always be here to help you."

"What do you mean?"

Hanna didn't answer. She just looked at the cigarette she held in her hand, and then she put it back in the packet and threw the packet in the bin.

"I've been thinking about quitting anyway," she said. "Now is as good a time as any."

"What do you mean, you won't always be here to help me?" I said.

Hanna looked at me and sighed. Maybe she was getting tired of me. Maybe she didn't want to be my friend any more.

"Basically," she said, "you need to toughen up. You don't have to *feel* tough. You just have to act like it."

I thought about this. What do people do when they want to act tough?

Hanna lifted up her backpack and put it over one of her shoulders. "I have to get to class," she said, and started walking towards the exit. "Are you coming or not?" she shouted as she hurried out the door. I picked up the packet of cigarettes from the bin before rushing after her. I figured they might come in handy.

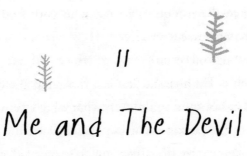

## 11

# Me and The Devil

It was a Tuesday and we were having Social Studies. We were cutting out pictures from magazines and gluing them to sheets of paper. On one sheet we glued pictures of things that we appreciated in today's society. On the other half, things we didn't appreciate. Our teacher, Harald Foss, taught second grade until last year. It shows in the assignments he gives us.

I took my stone out of my pencil case and held it inside my fist. Sometimes I take it out for a bit and just hold it. I like the way it feels in my hand.

I looked over at Frida, who was sitting on the other side of the room. Every now and then, she turned her head to talk to Julie Losvik. They were smiling and laughing.

And probably telling secrets. Then Frida tucked a lock of her perfect hair behind her ear and started to cut out pictures in the shape of a heart. How clever.

I went up to Harald's desk, which he had turned into a crafts table. He had laid out scissors, glue sticks, glitter and paper cut-outs in different shapes. There were also several magazines and newspapers for us to find pictures in. I looked at the table, but couldn't see anything that I liked. I ended up grabbing a paper cut-out shaped like a cat and a golden star, and then found my seat.

Shortly after, Harald said, "Okay, it's time to present your work to the rest of the class."

I looked down at my poster. It was empty.

"Who wants to go first?"

Frida smiled and raised her hand.

She held up one of her posters so the rest of the class could see. It was titled, *Things I do not like in our modern-day society*. She pointed to a picture of some chocolate-chip cookies. "These cookies contain palm oil. Every year, large areas of rainforest are cut down to make these kinds of oils. This endangers the lives of people and animals and has a huge impact on the climate. There are plenty of ways to make sweets without using palm oil, so I think this is unnecessary."

Frida smiled and pointed to a picture of a mink. "Minks

are killed every day to make fur. This is a very cruel industry and quite frankly animal abuse, if you ask me. They raise animals only to kill them so we can look nice."

Then she held up her second poster: *Things I like in our modern-day society.*

There was a picture of a family sitting at a table eating breakfast and another picture of three girls laughing, and a picture of a red house. She had also cut out some letters that spelled *home* and *family*. She had decorated the poster with silver stars and hearts and on the bottom corner of the poster she had glued a small round stone. On it she had written the word *Love* with permanent marker.

The stone was oval shaped, in a grey tone, and was covered in tiny black dots.

Frida started talking. I don't remember exactly what she said, but it was something about how the picture of the family represented love and happiness.

I grabbed my pencil case and shook it so I could see what was in there.

I couldn't see my stone.

I turned my pencil case upside down and emptied it on my desk.

Pens and pencils fell out, along with a ruler, two erasers and a pencil sharpener. But no stone. The stone was not there.

The stone was glued to Frida's poster and was written on in permanent ink.

Frida was saying something about how the picture of the red house made her feel safe and loved. Or maybe she was talking about her own house. I felt dizzy and confused. I think that might be why I blocked out most of what she said. I remember that her poster looked nice though. And I wondered what it would look like if someone were to cut it in half. Frida found her seat, still smiling, and another kid went up to present their work. I don't remember who it was. Maybe Gjermund Moen or Vegard Gudmestad. One of the boys from the back row.

What happened next is a bit of a blur. I remember getting up from my seat, holding my scissors, and I remember walking across the room. But it was like someone else was doing it. Like I was sitting in my seat and watching my body walk across the room. I think Gjermund or Vegard or whoever it was stopped talking. Or maybe the sudden loud screaming just drowned out all the other sounds.

The next thing I remember is everyone staring at me. And Frida looking at me with a mixture of confusion and anger. And Frida screaming and screaming and screaming.

Harald rushed over to me. "What the hell is going on?"

I looked at him.

"Malin!" he said. "Malin, what are you doing?"

I looked down at my hands. In one hand I was holding the scissors.

In the other, a handful of perfect brown hair.

"She took my stone!" I shouted. "It's mine and she took it!"

"What are you talking about?" Harald said.

Me, Frida and Harald were standing in the corridor. He'd taken us out of class so he could sort out what had happened. Meanwhile he'd got one of the substitute teachers to step in and take over the class. I could hear kids laughing and shouting on the other side of the door. It sounded like utter chaos in there.

"The stone on her poster," I whispered. "It's mine."

Harald looked over at Frida. "What stone?"

"I have no idea what she is talking about," Frida shouted. "I found the stone on the crafts table. It was just sitting there." She was holding her right hand to her head, covering the part where I cut her hair. "Who cares about a stupid stone anyway?" She looked at me. "You weirdo!" Then she started crying.

The school called Frida's parents and told them what had happened. And then they came and picked her up and she got the rest of the day off.

They called my parents too and asked them both to come in for an "emergency meeting with the principal". My dad even had to leave work early to be there.

I had never seen Principal Skogen so angry before. He said that what I had done was an assault. A violation. Illegal.

"If we were in America you would have been charged with assault with a lethal weapon at hand," he said.

My dad flinched. "Really?" he said.

Principal Skogen looked a bit startled. "I don't know. Probably." Then he raised his voice again. "More importantly, if Frida's parents decide to file a complaint, this could go on Malin's permanent record." My stomach was riding a roller coaster. Up and down, over and over again. I felt like throwing up.

I looked over at my mom and dad. Neither of them said much. My dad was making fists with both of his hands, and his knuckles were turning white. My mom held her handbag on her lap and smiled the way she does when she pretends that everything is okay.

Then Principal Skogen started talking about something called CAPS. Child and Adolescent Psychiatry Services. "I would strongly suggest that we get in touch with them for a follow-up," he said, looking at my parents. "In the first instance you would receive a letter calling Malin in for a meeting. No big deal, really. For now it would just help with mapping out the situation and getting some input on how to proceed further."

My dad was holding his right hand over his eyes, rubbing them slightly. I wasn't sure if he was listening to Principal Skogen. My mom still smiled, but was clenching her handbag in a tighter grip.

"I think we should discuss this further in private," Principal Skogen said. "I will call you."

Principal Skogen suspended me for the rest of the week, which meant that I would miss the trip to the museum. This was just as well, because I didn't feel like talking to anyone at school for a while.

When I got home I went to bed without dinner. I tried to remember when I last had the stone. I couldn't remember leaving it on the crafts table, but maybe I did. Frida had called me a weirdo for caring about a stone. And looking back at it now, it did seem childish and stupid.

Principal Skogen said that I had done something illegal. I didn't know what was scarier; the fact that Frida might report the incident to the police, or the fact that my dad hadn't yelled at me.

## 12

# Suspension

I wasn't allowed to go to school, so I stopped by Magnus's house. He'd called me and said that he had heard what happened and that I could come over if I wanted to, because he had the day off. I guessed my mom had told Aunt Lillian about it.

I rang his doorbell at 10.46 a.m. and we went into Magnus's room. He sat down by his desk and I sat down on his bed. He normally keeps his room much tidier than Sigve does. There were some clothes on the floor, but no leftover food or empty Coke bottles. Magnus had brought down an old record player from the attic and he was trying to make it work.

"I think I can get it running again if I replace the needle," Magnus said.

"How will you find music to play on it?"

"My mom has some old records. And I can find more in vintage shops."

"But you won't be able to find new music."

Magnus shrugged. "I am not really into mainstream music anyway. I like different things." He took up his phone and put on a song. "Like this," he said as the music filled the room. "It's Daniel Kvammen."

"A lot of people listen to Daniel Kvammen."

"Yeah, but I listened to him before he was popular."

We didn't say anything for a while. I was watching Magnus dust off the record player. He was stroking it like a dog or something. But a dog made of glass, which he was worried would break if he petted it too hard.

Then he said, "So you got suspended from school, huh?"

I nodded.

"Because you cut that girl's hair?"

I looked over at the shelf with all of Magnus's swimming trophies. They were not lined up nicely but stacked in front of each other and on top of each other. A few medals hung on a hook on the wall and some of them just lay in bundles on the shelf. It was like he had too many prizes and not enough room for them all.

"Do you think Frida is still mad at me?"

"Probably."

"I shouldn't have cut her hair."

"No," Magnus said. "But everyone screws up sometimes."

I thought about how I had made Frida cry. Maybe she wasn't the Devil after all. Maybe I was.

"Her hair will grow back," Magnus said.

Magnus wanted to practise holding his breath underwater again and asked if I could time him. In the bathroom he filled a bucket with water just like last time. He got down on his knees, took a deep breath and put his head in the bucket.

My mind went to Frida again. My dad had talked to her dad to smooth things over. Apparently they kind of know each other from way back. Everybody kind of knows everybody around here. Frida's dad agreed not to press charges, and my dad promised that I would apologize to her in person.

Magnus came up from the bucket and exhaled, dripping water everywhere. Then I realized that I had forgotten to press the timer.

He tried one more time, but he was kind of exhausted from his first try and he was only able to hold his breath for three minutes and fifty-nine seconds. That is not bad, but it wasn't a personal best.

84

"Principal Skogen said that I might get a letter from CAPS. To call me in for a meeting," I said.

"What's CAPS?"

"The Child and Adolescent Psychiatry Services."

"Okay."

"What will they talk to me about in the meeting?"

Magnus wiped his face with a towel. "I'm not sure," he said. "I never had one."

Magnus said that he would make me lunch. He warmed sausages in a pot of boiling water and made instant mashed potatoes. He finished the mash off by stirring in some seasoning packets meant for Maggi 3 Minute Noodles. "To spice it up," he said.

We sat down at the kitchen table to eat. The mash tasted horrible and wonderful all at the same time.

On the wall there were two pictures of Magnus as a child and Aunt Lillian. One where they were skiiing, and one where they were playing with a ball in the back yard. I wondered who had taken the pictures.

"Magnus, do you know who your dad is?" I said.

He looked puzzled. I had never asked him about this before because there never seemed to be a good time for questions like that.

"He shook his head. "No, I don't."

"Did you ask Aunt Lillian?"

"I used to ask her all the time when I was younger. She said he was a good man, but he couldn't be in my life due to certain circumstances."

"What circumstances?"

"I'm not sure. And I don't think it really matters." Magnus put more tomato sauce on his plate. "There is no excuse for abandoning your child if you ask me. I know I would never do that. No matter what."

And I knew Magnus wouldn't do anything like that because he is a really nice guy and it was hard to imagine his dad as a good man if he didn't stick around to take care of his own child.

"I think you'd make a good dad," I said.

He smiled. "Wouldn't take much to beat mine."

"Mine neither."

We laughed. "At least you got one," Magnus said.

After we finished our meal Magnus got up and put our plates in the sink.

"I have to apologize to Frida," I said. "Before I go back to school."

"I would do it as soon as possible."

"Really?"

"Yeah. It is better to get it over with."

\* \* \*

After visiting Magnus I cycled straight over to Frida's house to apologize. It was better to get it over with. Her dad opened the door, and even though I had given his daughter a new hairdo, he was actually nice to me. I asked for Frida and he went inside to get her while I waited on the doorstep. A couple of minutes later she came to the door, wearing a long knitted sweater. She had a new, much shorter haircut. It actually looked better than before.

"I am sorry for cutting your hair," I said.

Frida didn't say anything. She just looked at me as if she expected me to say something else. But I didn't know what else I should say. So I said the same thing again, "I am sorry for cutting your hair."

Frida crossed her arms and just as she opened her mouth to say something her dad showed up in the doorway. "Are you two still standing out here in the cold?" He turned to Frida. "Why don't you invite your friend in for a snack?"

I had no idea why he was calling me her friend.

Everything in Frida's house was white. The sofa, the picture frames and the bookshelves. And on the window sill were four wooden letters that spelled out *home*. I sat down on the white couch and Frida brought me a glass of water with a slice of cucumber in it and put an open jar of olives on the table. Then she put on a DVD, before sitting down on the other end of the sofa. The DVD was a documentary about an animal I had never seen before: the alligator snapping turtle. The narrator said that the alligator snapping turtle is found primarily in south-eastern United States waters. It is one of the heaviest freshwater turtles in the world and got its name because of its powerful jaws and its shell that is similar to the skin of an alligator.

Without taking her eyes away from the TV, Frida said, "Do you know how the alligator snapping turtle catches its prey?"

I said I didn't.

"As it is a turtle, it can't chase after prey at high speed. So it just lies in the water with its mouth wide open." She held out her hands to represent its jaws. "And then it just has to wait until prey comes. Fish, insects and sometimes even frogs. They swim right into the turtle's mouth. And then, when they least expect it, the turtle snaps its jaws shut –" Frida clapped her hands together – "killing the prey instantly."

Frida kept staring at the screen. "I guess they deserve to die. If they are stupid enough to swim right into the snapping turtle's mouth, I mean. Don't you agree?" She turned and looked at me. Her eyes seemed lifeless. Like two small stones pushed into a snowman's head.

I began to think that I would never make it out of there alive. I was on death row and my last meal was an olive and a glass of cucumber water.

Then her dad came back in. "Oh, you are watching the alligator snapping turtle," he said. "That's a great documentary."

I said I had to go and ran out of the house and cycled home as fast as I could. I knew it wouldn't be this easy. Frida was the queen and you don't mess with the queen without there being consequences.

When I got home I checked the postbox. It was full of bills and advertisements, but no letter from CAPS.

I went inside and lay down on my bed and hoped that Monday would never come. Oscar came in and curled up at the foot of my bed. He always looks like he doesn't have a care in the world. And I guess he doesn't. It must be nice to be a cat.

## 13

# Expecting

Hanna told me once that girls can get free contraceptive pills from the age of sixteen to twenty. It's no big deal at all. You don't have to have a gynaecological examination or anything. You can just talk to your doctor about it. Or even the school nurse (who is in every other Thursday) can prescribe them to you.

That's what she told me.

Hanna knew all this but somehow she got pregnant anyway. I was sitting on a chair in her room and she lay on her bed and stared at the ceiling and she told me that she was pregnant. The thought of a baby growing inside Hanna's stomach seemed impossible.

"My mom says I need to have an abortion. And my dad

of course agrees with everything she says." Hanna looked at me, and her voice became more intense. "An abortion! Can you believe it?" She looked back at the ceiling and said quietly, "It's almost seven weeks old already. It has a brain and a beating heart." She whispered, "It is a life."

It was weird and grotesque hearing Hanna talking about an abortion. But if she didn't have an abortion, that meant she would have a baby. At sixteen. And that didn't seem much better. But I suspected I shouldn't say that, so instead I said, "Who's the father?"

Hanna looked at me and raised one eyebrow. "It's Patrik, you moron! Who else would it be?"

I just wanted to make sure, but I guess you are not supposed to ask.

"Well, what does he say about it?" I said.

"I haven't told him yet."

Then she started crying. She put a heart-shaped cushion over her face and sobbed into it like a little child.

I looked around the room. Her Winnie the Pooh clock was ticking loudly on her dresser. It showed the time as 3.40, which was incorrect. The time was actually 3.43. Hanna told me once that her grandfather had given her that clock years ago, not long before he died, and she didn't have the heart to get rid of it. How could someone with a Winnie the Pooh clock and a bed full of heart-shaped cushions be about to become a mom?

Hanna sat up on her bed and removed the cushion from her face. Her mascara was smudged around her eyes and ran down her face in dark inky lines. Somehow she seemed to be aware of this without looking in a mirror, as she picked up some tissues from her bedside table and started wiping her face.

She threw the darkened tissues in the bin, picked up some new ones and continued to wipe her face.

A single tear ran from Hanna's eye, creating a new dark line that slowly made its way down her cheek.

I wanted to tell Hanna that everything was going to be okay, but how could I get her to believe that when I wasn't sure I believed it myself?

Hanna suddenly started laughing really loud. "I can't believe you actually cut Frida's hair," she said. "That's crazy. You're crazy."

I thought about Frida and how upset she had been. I didn't understand how Hanna could laugh about it. I wondered what everyone else at school thought about it. Maybe they were all mad at me now.

"Ruben accidentally broke my mom's porcelain giraffe," I said, mostly to change the subject.

"How did she take it?"

I shrugged. "She hasn't noticed yet."

Hanna didn't comment on that. Instead she put both of her hands on her tummy. "I'm thinking of keeping it." She lay down on her back again and looked at the ceiling. "It will be okay," she said. "I will be okay."

I got home at 4.26 p.m. and I saw that someone was waiting for me on my doorstep. It was Ruben. When he noticed me he smiled, making his crooked front tooth appear.

"Your mom said you were out so I decided to wait for you here," he said. "I hope that's okay."

"It is." I smiled.

"Good."

"I lost your stone," I said.

At first he looked a bit confused. Then he smiled and said, "Oh, that's okay."

"Yeah, I mean it was just a stone anyway."

He stopped smiling and shrugged. "Sure."

Then he reached inside his coat and took out a really old-looking book. He handed it to me and said, "Look what I got."

On the cover was a picture of three boys playing Monopoly. They were all wearing white shirts and braces and looked like little men. It was titled *101 Activities for Rainy Days*.

"It has a lot of really cool old games in it," Ruben said. He took out a small pouch from his jeans pocket. "Wanna play marbles?"

We needed a smooth surface to play on, so we went into the garage. I found a piece of chalk and Ruben drew a circle in the middle of the floor. Then he drew a line on each side of the circle and we sat down next to each other.

But the floor was too cold so we got a couple of logs that we keep stacked by one of the walls. We placed them on the floor and sat down.

Ruben started lining up the marbles inside the circle. "Everyone is talking at school," he said. "About how you cut Frida's hair."

I shuddered. "They are?" Nervously I asked, "What are they saying?"

He shrugged. "Just that. That you cut her hair."

"Oh."

"I don't get what the big deal is, her hair still looks good." He paused. "I mean, if you like that kind of hair, that is. I think curls are better."

I felt him looking at me, but I kept staring at the marbles in the circle. My cheeks were burning and my fingers felt like ice.

Ruben held up a slightly bigger marble. "Do you want to go first?"

I shook my head. "You go," I whispered.

We took turns shooting the big marble at the ones inside the circle. I didn't do too badly, but Ruben was a lot better at it and he won.

After the game, Ruben said, "So why did you do it?"

"Do what?"

"Cut Frida's hair."

I couldn't tell him the truth. It was too dumb.

I looked at him. "Why did you try and burn down the garage that time?"

Ruben thought for a while. "I think it was mostly two things. One was that my mom said that I couldn't get *Titanfall 2* for my Xbox and I was mad at her."

"And the other?"

He looked at me. "I had never seen a garage burn before."

And that's when Ruben kissed me. All of a sudden he just leaned in and quickly gave me a peck on the lips. His lips were cold, but the kiss felt warm. I didn't get the chance to follow the instructions from Google, because it was over just as soon as it started. My cheeks felt flaming hot and I held my icy hands up to my face to try and cool it down.

Then suddenly the garage door started opening. The sound startled us and we both jumped to our feet. My dad was home from work. Ruben and I quickly collected the marbles so that he wouldn't drive over them with his car.

I said goodbye to Ruben and went inside with my dad.

For dinner we were having roast pork. As we all sat down at the table, my mom asked me if I could get her a carving knife from the drawer.

Sigve threw his hands up in the air. "Wow, are you crazy?" Then he got up from his seat. "I'll get it. I think we all know that it is not safe to let Malin handle sharp objects."

"Stop it," my mom said.

My dad sighed. "Let's just eat."

I didn't care what anybody said. All I could think of was Ruben and how for a brief moment his cold, soft lips had touched mine.

# 14

# Fortunes and Misfortunes

It was a Sunday, which meant that the next day was a Monday. That's usually how it goes, but this time it was a little bit different. This Monday was my first day back at school after being suspended and I was feeling anxious.

I was in the living room, watching an interview with Vanja Haraldsen, one of the *Norwegian Idol* contestants. They asked her what she did to relax. She said that when she was a child she used to watch cartoons, but now she would normally have a glass of red wine. My mom does relax a lot after drinking wine so it could be true. But I am too young to drink and too old for cartoons.

Then my mom came in and announced that we were all going out for lunch.

There are only two things that are open in Haasund on Sundays. Holberg's shop and the Chinese restaurant, *Haasund Kina Kjøkken*. We don't really have many family outings when there is no special occasion, so I was a little surprised to learn that we were all going out for Chinese food together. Even Sigve came along, and he is usually too cool to hang out with us in public.

As we walked to the restaurant, I decided that I wanted to try the Peking duck. I had never eaten duck before.

Everything in *Haasund Kina Kjøkken* is either red or gold, except for the chairs and tables, which are black. At least, I think the tables are black. They are always covered with red tablecloths, so I'm not sure. On the walls are framed pictures of some Chinese writing, and on the counter sits one of those Chinese lucky cat figurines that waves. I read somewhere that these figurines are actually from Japan, so I have no idea why we call them "Chinese lucky cats" or why they would have them in a Chinese restaurant.

We were the only ones in the restaurant, but we still had to wait to be seated. As we stood in the doorway and looked at the empty room, my dad sighed loudly several times and kept checking his watch.

"Maybe we should just go," he said.

I looked at my mom to see if she agreed, but my mom said, "Calm down, Leif. We are not in a rush."

And then the man came over and smiled and showed us to a table near the window. He gave us four menus and asked what drinks we wanted. I asked my mom if I could order a Coke and she said yes. While we waited for our drinks, I asked my mom if I could order the Peking duck and she said yes to that as well. I didn't know what was going on, but I liked it. My mom picked up the menu and started flipping through the pages. This is the only place we go to for special occasions – sometimes for birthdays and sometimes for Mother's Day, but never on a regular Sunday. Sigve and my dad always order the same – fried rice with chicken and vegetables – so they didn't need to look at a menu. While we waited, no one was talking. Sigve was playing with some chopsticks in the sugar bowl and my dad was tapping his foot so hard that the table was shaking. I couldn't see my mom's face because it was hidden behind the menu.

The man brought us our drinks and asked if we were ready to order, but my mom said that we needed a couple more minutes. The man smiled and nodded and walked away. Then my mom put down the menu and said that she had some news that she wanted to share with us. My dad stopped tapping his foot and cleared his throat and leaned forward in his chair, like he was the one who had news to tell.

My mom said, "It was actually the reason I suggested coming here today."

Sigve put down the chopsticks. "I also have something to share," he said. "Can I go first?"

My mom glanced at my dad before turning to Sigve. "Of course you can."

Sigve looked at the table. He picked up one of the chopsticks and circled it around the tablecloth. "I've got a job at the Coop in Bryne. On the checkout."

"Oh, well that's nice," my mom said.

"I've had it for six months. Full-time."

"What are you talking about? You are still in school."

"I haven't been for a while. And I am not going back."

"The hell you are!" my dad kicked in.

"Wouldn't make a difference," Sigve said. "I've missed so much school already, they won't let me take any of my exams."

Everyone became quiet. The Chinese cat from Japan kept waving its paw like nothing had happened. Then my dad hit his fist on the table so hard that my mom's glass of fizzy water got knocked over, and then he got up and walked out the door. The waiter rushed over to clean up the mess and my mom ordered a glass of wine.

And then my mom took a picture of me and Sigve where it looked like we were having fun and uploaded it to Facebook. Sigve asked my mom what her news was, but she said she didn't want to talk about it without my dad. And then she ordered fried rice with chicken and vegetables for everybody. It didn't really matter because I wasn't really hungry any more. I kept thinking that I had to go back to school the next day and I didn't feel ready to face everyone. I asked my mom if I could stay home from school just one more day, but she said no. I told her that I really could use one more day of rest because I had a bit of a sore throat, but she said no again.

After we had finished our meal the waiter brought the bill on a plate together with three fortune cookies. I opened one of them and took out the little note and unfolded it. It said, *Things will get worse before they get better.*

My dad never came back to the restaurant, so after my mom had paid the bill the three of us walked home. I was angry with my mom for not letting me stay home from school, so I gave her the silent treatment the rest of the day. I guess it would have been more effective if she had noticed.

# 15

# Back to School

Haasund Lower Secondary School looked the same as it always had. Not that it should have looked any different. After all, it was only five days since I'd last set foot in those halls.

Before I went in, I stood by the bike racks and watched all the kids walk up the steps and through the entrance. They were joking and laughing like it was just another day. Everything looked the same, but somehow it felt different. Then I started to worry that class would start before I made it to my desk, so I hurried past the courtyard and through the door.

It looked the same on the inside as well. Except for one thing. There were posters on the walls with pictures of Frida, Julie and Norunn with a headline that said, *Vote for your favourite prom queen.* So the prom was happening after all.

I sat down at my desk just as the bell rang. We were having Norwegian class with Trude Fjell and she said that we were going to analyze a short story named "Karen". That included finding underlying themes and metaphors, which I don't really understand or see the point of doing.

Like that poem by Inger Hagerup, where it says something about how when it is time to take your final boat trip you have to leave all your luggage behind. Trude said that this meant that when you die it doesn't matter how rich you are or how many things you own. What matters is what kind of a person you were. I think that if this is what Inger Hagerup meant, she should have just said so.

After we read through the story, we had to answer some questions. Like, *What sort of parallel stories do we find within this story?* and, *What does the wind symbolize?* These kinds of tasks don't have any real right or wrong answers. Still Trude will normally tell me that I am doing it wrong and I find it very confusing.

I spent the rest of the class doodling in my notebook. I looked over at Frida. She seemed to write a lot. She is usually very good at these things.

At recess I went to the toilets behind the gym to meet Hanna. She still goes there to hang out sometimes, even though she doesn't smoke any more. Hanna told me that she was working up the courage to tell Patrik about the baby. I didn't know what to say to that so I asked her about the prom instead. She said that it was to be held at the end of March. Apparently, after I cut Frida's hair, people gave her a lot of money. And now Frida and her friends can have their dream ball. So it seemed like something good came out of this whole thing.

"She should be thanking you," Hanna laughed.

On my way back to my classroom I noticed that some kids were talking but when I approached they stopped and just stared at me. As I walked past them I heard someone whispering, "She is such a weirdo."

It was a new feeling to have people talk about me. But it was also quite a new feeling to have a friend to meet up with. So going to school that day made me feel bad, but also good.

When the final bell rang I stayed in my seat until everyone else had left the room. Then I got up and slowly made my way out the door. Hanna was waiting for me in the courtyard and we cycled home together without saying much. On Egeland Street we parted ways and I waved to her before she disappeared around the curve.

When I got home, Sigve was sitting at the kitchen table drinking chocolate milk. He was wearing red Coop work clothes.

"I thought the Coop in Bryne had a blue uniform?" I said.

"I work in Haasund now." He pointed at the milk carton. "Do you want some?"

"Okay," I said.

I sat down at the table and he poured me a glass. I couldn't remember the last time me and my big brother were in the kitchen drinking chocolate milk together.

Then Sigve said, "Thanks for not telling Mom and Dad about my job, but I actually could use my access card back."

"What access card?"

"It's no big deal, I am not mad. They gave me a new one and everything. It's just that if I don't give the other one back they will charge me for it."

"I didn't take it. I didn't know anything about your job."

"Then where's my card?"

"I don't know."

Sigve seemed calm and not filled with his usual rage. Instead he was actually listening to what I said. And maybe that's why he believed me.

"I suppose I could have lost it," he said.

Sigve loses his things a lot.

"Well, thanks anyway," he said and got up to leave.

"Don't mention it."

Just as he was about to walk out of the room he turned around. "Oh, right," he said. "You owe me a hundred kroner."

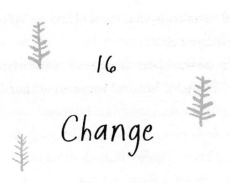

# 16

# Change

Sigve wanted money that I no longer had, so I went around the house searching for loose change. First I went into the living room and turned over the cushions on the sofa. I found a hairpin, two pens and a knitting needle. And under the sofa I found three kroner that I put in my pocket.

Then I went into the laundry room to see if any change had fallen out in the washing machine. In the machine I found a toothpick, a five-kroner coin and a pack of gum that was gooey and gross. I put the coin in my pocket and left the toothpick and the gum in the machine.

It was only 2.44 p.m. so my dad wouldn't be home from work for at least one hour and fifty minutes. His work hours are 8 a.m. to 4 p.m. and his drive home is about eighteen minutes, but he is never home at 4.18. Sometimes there is traffic and sometimes he needs to work longer. He normally comes home from work somewhere between 4.34 and 5.49 p.m. So I decided to check his study. I didn't want to poke around too much because I was worried that I would move things around and that my dad would see that I had been in there. But I decided that I could check his desk drawers. I imagined that that was a place where people would keep change. I opened up the top drawer. It only contained pens, pencils, Post-it pads and a pencil sharpener.

In the next drawer there was a bunch of papers and on top of them was a stack of old photographs that I had never seen before. I picked up a black-and-white photo of a young man in a suit. He was looking straight into the camera with no smile, kind eyes and curly hair. I turned it around and on the back it said *Alfred Sande*. That was my dad's dad. My grandfather. I didn't know my grandfather had curly hair. I didn't even know he ever had hair.

I let my fingers run through my own curls. As he had short hair, his curls were probably more manageable than mine.

At 3.21 p.m. Hanna called and said she wanted to talk to me, so I went to her house. When I saw her she looked really happy. I hadn't seen her smile like that in weeks.

"I have talked to Patrik," she said. "I am keeping the baby."

"But what about your mom?" I said. "I thought she decided you should…"

"Should what?"

"You know."

"I've looked into it," she said. "She can't force me."

She told me that she and Patrik had a plan. She would tell her mom that she would have an abortion, just to get her off her back for a while. She might even lie and say that she had gone through with the abortion, but she wasn't really sure if her mom would believe her. "I'll think of something," she said. "I just have to make it to week twelve, because then it will be difficult to do anything about it."

"Why week twelve?"

Hanna raised one eyebrow. "Did your year skip sex education or something?"

"What do you mean?"

"It is much harder to get an abortion after week twelve."

Hanna also told me that once Patrik finished his second year of upper secondary school, he would get a placement at a plumbing company and then they could get their own flat.

I didn't say anything, but it didn't seem like Hanna needed me to. She closed her eyes and smiled. "What do you think about Emma?" she said.

"What?"

"Emma is a nice name for a girl, don't you think?"

When I got home my dad wasn't back from work yet and my mom was taking a nap, even though it was nearly dinner time. I decided to continue my search for loose change. I remembered that I hadn't checked the dryer, so I went into the laundry room again. But there was no change in the dryer, just a bottle of red wine. The label said, *Make Every Day a Holiday*. I wondered if I should put the bottle in the kitchen where it belonged, but decided to leave it where it was. My mom would know where to find it. I shut the door of the dryer and went into my room. I reached into my pocket and took out the money I had collected. Together with the money I had in my piggy bank, I had exactly twenty-one kroner.

The next day Hanna wasn't at school. I looked for her in the toilets behind the gym but she wasn't there. Then I walked over to her classroom but I couldn't see her anywhere.

"Are you looking for Hanna?" a voice said.

It was a boy I'd never seen before, but he seemed to know who I was.

I nodded.

"She is home sick today," he said. And then he walked off.

I sent Hanna a text and asked if she was okay. Two minutes and thirteen seconds later she replied, *Morning sickness. Sometimes it lasts all day.* And she ended it with a smiley face. She made it seem like morning sickness was something that was completely natural for her to have.

A lot of the kids were still whispering about me when I walked back to my classroom. It seemed even worse now that I didn't have Hanna to turn to.

On my way home from school I saw Frida and some of her friends on the corner of Torg Street and Sentrum Street. I wasn't sure if I felt comfortable walking past them and was considering going back and taking a detour. But Frida had already spotted me. And all of a sudden she started to make her way over. That made me feel uneasy. I thought about what Hanna had said about sticking up for myself: *You don't have to feel tough. You just have to act it.*

I quickly reached into my backpack and took out the packet of cigarettes that Hanna had thrown in the bin.

I put a cigarette in my mouth and lit it. They didn't make me too dizzy that time. The trick was not to inhale.

Frida approached me and said, "I just wanted to tell you something."

I looked at her.

"I forgive you," she said. "You know, for cutting my hair. I forgive you."

I blew out smoke from the side of my mouth. "You do?"

"Sure. I think I have to be the bigger person. It can't be easy for you, with your mom and all."

Now that was a really weird thing to say, because my mom was fine.

"Seriously." She held out her hand. "Truce?"

And so the Devil shook the hand of a civilian. I just didn't know which was which any more.

# 17

# Friendship

During the week Hanna kept not showing up at school due to being sick. Sometimes she would come in later, or leave earlier. And sometimes she just wouldn't show up at all.

She did tell me once that she wouldn't always be around to protect me. Maybe this was what she meant.

When the bell rang for our lunch break at 11.03 a.m., all the kids immediately gathered in their groups as usual. After I had eaten my ham and cheese sandwich, I decided to go and get some fresh air. I stood on the steps in front of the main entrance and watched the kids in the courtyard. They were all in their regular groups too. The kids who like football in one group. The kids who skateboard in another.

Then I saw Ruben. He was crossing the courtyard, heading in my direction.

When he saw me he stopped and smiled.

"Hello, Malin," he said.

"Hello."

"What's up?"

I shrugged. "Nothing."

I noticed that someone had put up a poster about the prom on the main door.

"Are you going to the prom?" I said.

"Probably," he said. "I guess if everyone else is going, I will too. I mean I think these kinds of things are a bit silly."

"But you supported Frida's campaign."

Ruben looked confused. "What do you mean?"

Then someone opened the front door and called Ruben's name. It was one of his friends.

"I've got to go," Ruben said. "We should hang out again soon."

"Okay."

"If you want to."

"Yes."

"Oh, you have something in your hair," Ruben said. He reached out his arm and let his index finger and thumb slide down a lock of my hair. He held up a tiny bit of white dust to show me what he'd removed, before throwing it away.

Then his friend called him again and Ruben said, "I will talk to you soon," and went inside. Through the glass door I watched them walk away. I waited to see if Ruben would turn around and wave at me. He didn't, but I guessed it was still okay. After all, he had already said, "I will talk to you soon," which can be counted as a goodbye.

Suddenly I heard someone calling my name. It was Frida and she was waving me over to her group.

I decided to go over to her. I was on good terms with Frida at the moment and I wanted to keep it that way.

"Hey," Frida said.

"Hello."

"How's it going?"

"Good."

"So why are you not with that friend of yours?" Norunn said. "The one with all the mascara and the grey beanie hat."

"She is not in school today."

"I haven't seen her in ages," Julie said.

"She has been sick a lot."

"Sick?"

"I think it is morning sickness. Sometimes it lasts all day."

Norunn and Julie let out a slight gasp and they all quickly exchanged looks.

Frida was grinning. "What did you say?"

I didn't answer.

"She's pregnant?"

I didn't say anything and Frida and her friends didn't ask any more questions. They just smiled. And then the bell rang.


When I got home from school the door was locked so I figured no one was home. I let myself in and as soon as I grabbed the door handle, Oscar jumped out of a bush and came running towards me. He always seems to know when we are home.

After I fed Oscar I sat down at the kitchen table and started on my homework. Just as I was about to finish up my English work I heard a coughing sound coming from my parents' bedroom. I went and opened the door to see who it was. My mom was lying in bed, sleeping. I figured she had another headache, because she does take naps in the middle of the day when she gets them. I closed the door as gently as I could so that I didn't make any noise.

At 4.46 p.m. my dad came home from work. He walked into the kitchen carrying today's post.

"Hello," he said, and started to go through the envelopes he held in his hands.

"Hello."

"Where is your mom?"

"She is taking a nap."

"Really?" He sighed and ran his hand through his hair. "All right," he said. "I will tell Sigve to pick up Chinese food on his way home from work."

"What's in the post?" I said.

"Mostly bills, I think. Why do you ask?"

"I am waiting for the letter from CAPS."

"Don't worry about that."

"What do you mean?"

My dad looked at me. "We are not going to talk to strangers about our stuff. It's nobody's business."

# 18

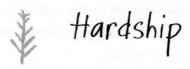

Hardship

The next day a lot of kids were gossiping and whispering in my school. But this time it wasn't about me. They all seemed to be talking about a girl from the tenth grade. The one with the leather jacket and the grey beanie. The one who was pregnant.

"What did you do?" Hanna was blocking the entrance to the toilets behind the gym. She stared at me with dark eyes and she didn't blink.

"What do you mean?"

"You told them. You told everyone."

"Told everyone what?"

"That I am pregnant, stupid. What else?"

Her words cut like a razor blade and she looked like

she wanted to kill something.

I looked at the ground. "But I didn't."

"Apart from Patrik, you were the only one who knew. You must have told someone."

"No. But I was talking to Frida and…"

"Frida? Are you being serious?" she scoffed. "Of all the people to talk to about anything, you decided that Frida was a good option?"

I didn't answer.

Hanna shook her head. "I really don't know if you would do something like this on purpose, or if you are just that stupid."

Then she walked away. But she didn't walk back into the building. She rushed across the courtyard and through the main gate, leaving school grounds.

I definitely didn't do it on purpose. So I guessed that meant I was stupid.

At lunch break I went to the courtyard and took out the encyclopedia I had in my bag. I half-heartedly flipped through the pages. It felt lonely to be on my own again. Hanna had been away from school a lot lately, but this time she wasn't gone because she was sick. She was gone because she was mad at me, and that felt different.

I saw Ruben standing by the bike racks. He was laughing and talking to his friends. I wondered if I should go up to him, but he seemed busy.

"Do you like him or something?"

I looked up. Frida and Julie were standing next to me.

"What?" I said.

Frida nodded towards Ruben. "Ruben. Do you like him?"

"No."

This wasn't entirely true. Normally I don't tell lies, but her question threw me and the answer just fell out.

"I think he likes you," Julie said. And then they walked off.

How could she know? Both of them always seemed to know everything.

I didn't feel like going straight home after school so I walked over to Magnus's house instead. He finishes class early on Thursdays.

Magnus said he had something to show me in the garage. He opened the door and pointed at an orange moped. It was the one from the picture he had shown me a while back.

He stroked the moped with his hand and continued down over the seat. "Check out the great condition it's in."

I looked but I couldn't see what he saw. To me, it still looked like a piece of junk.

"It's going to need a bit of work before I can ride it though," Magnus said. "Guess how much it was?"

I shrugged. "I don't know."

"Only 2500 kroner."

I couldn't believe that he had paid that much for it.

"Which is good news for you too," Magnus said.

"Why?"

"My mom said that since it was so cheap, I could also have a new phone."

He reached into the pocket of his jeans and pulled out a thin black smartphone, and held it out for me to see. It looked exactly like the one he had before.

"Which means that you can have my old phone."

"But I already have a phone."

"Yes, but this one is better."

We went inside and Magnus put my SIM card into his old phone – my new phone – and connected it to Wi-Fi. We downloaded some apps – Facebook, Instagram and Snapchat – and some games – Jelly Splash, Wordfeud and Candy Crush.

Magnus handed me the phone and I put it in my pocket.

"Hanna is mad at me," I said.

"Your friend?"

I nodded. "She thinks I told everyone that she is pregnant."

"Is she?"

"Yes, but I didn't tell anyone."

"Then why does she think you did?"

I shrugged. "I only told Frida that Hanna wasn't in school because of morning sickness, but I didn't say she was pregnant."

Magnus frowned. "I don't know if you can have one without the other."

A while back Magnus had told me that everyone screws up sometimes. But I seemed to be the only one who did that these days.

"How do I make it better?"

"I think all you can do is apologize and hope that she understands that you didn't mean to hurt her. If you are true friends, eventually she will forgive you."

Magnus asked me if I wanted to stay for dinner and I looked at the time. It was 4.49 p.m. already, which surprised me. I'm usually very good at keeping track of time. I said, "I think I'd better go."

When I got home I could hear my dad's loud voice as soon as I stepped into the hallway. He sounded really mad this time.

I peeked inside the living room. I saw my dad was standing by the coffee table, shouting at Sigve. I couldn't see my mom anywhere, but that didn't surprise me. She hardly ever gets involved in the heavy things any more.

"You are going back to school next year!" my dad yelled.

"Why?" Sigve sat in one of the armchairs, looking completely chilled.

"Why? So you can get a proper education and a decent job."

"I like my job."

"You like it now! What if you wake up in ten years and wish you had an education?"

"Then in ten years I will get an education."

"For fuck's sake!" my dad yelled and punched the wall.

Immediately he covered his right fist with his left hand and let out a muffled scream. "Now look what you made me do."

I backed out of the house and closed the door behind me. Then I went into the garage and sat down on a chair and played some games on my new phone. I also sent Hanna a text to say that I was sorry, but she didn't reply.

# 19

# Physical Education

Of all the subjects we have in school, PE is my least favourite. I especially dislike any sports that involve a ball. I always seem to be in the wrong place at the wrong time, and the few times that I am in the right place, I don't know what to do with the ball. I have conveniently "forgotten" my PE kit a lot this year. They can't make you do PE if you don't bring a change of clothes. In fact I have left my kit at home so many times that my teacher, Haakon Krag, told me that if I missed one more class, he would have to fail me.

We have PE every Tuesday and Thursday in the fourth and fifth periods. This Tuesday we were playing volleyball. Haakon picked out Gjermund Moen and Vegard Gudmestad as team captains, as per normal. The rest of the class lined up against the wall while they picked their teams. One by one, I watched Kjetil, Sivert, Frida, Julia and the others being chosen.

Then only me, Otto Njaa and Sondre Håland were left. Otto has this nervous twitch in his left arm and can be quite unpredictable when handling a ball. Sondre is very tall and skinny and, like me, quite clumsy. He has long limbs that should work well in games like volleyball, but for some reason they don't.

I don't really know them that well, but I would guess that PE is their least favourite subject too. Gjermund and Vegard looked at each other like they were facing the biggest problem in their life so far.

"Okay," Vegard said, "I will take Otto and you can have the other two." And with that, it was settled. We all went to our teams; Haakon blew his whistle and then the game started.

Most of the time during volleyball I stand in one spot and hope the ball doesn't come my way. If it does come my way I usually put my arms up to cover my face. Personally I don't care what happens to the ball, but the rest of my class seem to think it's pretty important that it makes it to the other side of the net. So if I mess up, people get mad and I don't like people being mad at me.

I kept checking my watch. It took six minutes and nineteen seconds before the ball came my way. I ducked and the ball hit the floor and bounced outside the thick white line that marks the volleyball court. A collective sigh sounded from my team while the other team cheered and high-fived each other. Haakon blew his whistle and held out his left arm to signal a point to the other team. "Malin, you are supposed to hit the ball!" Haakon yelled. "We're not playing dodgeball."

Then it was my turn to serve the ball. That is the worst part of volleyball, because that is the one moment when I can't pretend to be invisible. I actually have to try my best to get the ball over the net while all eyes are on me.

I went and stood behind the line with the ball in my hand. I bounced the ball a couple of times like I'd seen the others do. Then I threw the ball up in the air with my left hand while holding my right hand up next to my head, ready to shoot the ball towards the net. But I missed and it just bounced a couple of times on the floor before rolling under the net. My team sighed and moaned and rolled their eyes. They acted like they were surprised.

Then I had to do it again. "Watch the ball," Haakon said. And I did. I watched the ball as I threw it up in the air and when it was in position I hit it with my right hand. I didn't miss it this time. Not only did I hit it, it actually went the way it was supposed to go. But as my hand made contact with the ball I heard a pop in my right shoulder. Sudden pain shot down my arm and I dropped to the floor as the ball flew across the room. Then it hit the net and bounced back to our side of the court.

My arm hurt so much. And this time I knew what was wrong. I sat up and put my left hand under my right elbow for support as I started crying. I couldn't help it. I didn't want to go through this again. All the waiting time. All the pain.

Haakon rushed over to see what was wrong. I told him that I had dislocated my shoulder and he ran and got the emergency kit. He took out an instant cold pack, which he squeezed and rubbed for a couple of seconds before holding it out to me. "Put this on your shoulder," he said.

But I told him I couldn't because I was using my left hand to support my right arm. So he called one of the other kids over. "Otto," he yelled. "Come give me a hand." Haakon told Otto to hold the cold pack against my shoulder and ran out of the room. "I'll be right back," he called. I looked at Otto and hoped he wouldn't make any sudden moves.

All the kids were still staying in their allocated spots on the volleyball court. Some looking at me. Some looking at the floor. But they didn't move from their spots. They just stood there like they were glued to the floor. I stopped crying, because I knew that if I started sobbing it would hurt more.

After a little while Haakon came rushing back with Principal Skogen. Haakon told me that he had called my parents and that he would drive me to the medical centre. He hadn't been able to reach my mom but my dad would meet us there.

We went out to the parking lot, Haakon walking in front and holding the doors open. I felt nervous. "Mine is the red Toyota Corolla," he said. That didn't mean much to me, but there was only one red car in the parking lot so I headed towards that. I walked very slowly while Haakon nervously jogged in front. I didn't know why he was rushing. My dad works in an insurance company in Bryne and it takes eighteen minutes for him to drive to Haasund. So I knew we'd have to wait anyway.

Haakon held the car door open for me as I got in the passenger seat. I couldn't put my seat belt on because I had no free arm, so Haakon leaned over to help me. I held my breath to avoid taking in the smell of garlic he always reeks of. A lock of his greyish hair was sweaty and stuck to his forehead.

He finally buckled my belt and shut the door. Then he ran around the car and got behind the wheel.

On the floor of his car there was a bunch of empty Coke bottles that rolled backwards and forwards over my feet as he started driving. The smell from three air fresheners dangling from the mirror mixed with the smell of garlic – it made me feel sick.

The movement of the car made the pain worse and when Haakon hit a bump in the parking lot, I screamed. Loud.

Haakon looked at me nervously. "I'm sorry," he said. Then he hit another bump.

The medical centre is a three-minute drive from Haasund Lower Secondary School. It is a ten-minute walk if you cut through the park. I would have preferred to walk.

To get to the medical centre we had to make four turns. One to get out of the parking lot at my school, one at the roundabout, one to get on to Berg Street, and one to drive into the parking lot of the medical centre. At every turn I screamed at the top of my lungs. It felt as if my arm was being ripped from my body. Haakon kept apologizing, which, for some reason, made the experience even worse. If I had walked through the park I wouldn't have had to deal with any of this.

After three minutes and forty-nine seconds of a hell ride that smelled like garlic, watermelon, vanilla and raspberry car freshener, I could get out of the car – once Haakon helped me unbuckle my seat belt by leaning over me again.

The waiting room was completely empty and behind the desk there was a new receptionist. She was quite young, had brown hair and a nose piercing shaped like a heart. She was pretty.

I went to sit down in one of the chairs and soon Haakon came and sat down in the seat opposite mine. He tapped his foot and fiddled with his keys. "We have to wait until your dad gets here," he said.

I already knew that.

"What's your favourite subject in school?" he asked.

I didn't answer, and he didn't say anything else.

After eighteen minutes and twelve seconds my dad walked in. He nodded and smiled at the receptionist before saying hello to me. Haakon got out of his chair and shook his hand. "Thanks for coming in," he said.

"Of course." My dad smiled and quickly glanced over at the receptionist. He raised his voice slightly as he said, "No work is more important than your child."

The doctor wasn't the same as last time either. He was much younger and didn't listen to me when I said that I wasn't able to take my shirt off. "That shirt has to come off, even if we have to cut it off," he said.

A nurse cut my shirt, and helped me into a hospital gown. Then they took X-rays, even though they knew what was wrong with me. After studying the X-rays together with a nurse, the doctor finally gave me painkillers and pulled my shoulder back into place, before putting my arm in a sling.

Afterwards, the doctor wanted to talk to my dad and we both went into his office. He said that if you dislocate a joint at a young age, in fifty per cent of cases it will happen again. And again. He said that in a few weeks, once I got my sling off, I would need physiotherapy to help me recover and build up muscles in my arm to keep it from happening again. Stronger muscles would help my shoulder to stay in place.

If the problem continued we would discuss surgery, but for now physiotherapy would suffice.

"How much will that cost?" my dad said.

When we came back to the waiting room, Haakon was still there.

He and my dad shook hands again. "Thanks for sticking around," my dad said.

"Of course." Haakon glanced over at the receptionist. "We always have our students' best interests at heart."

Haakon said that I didn't have to come back to school so my dad said that he would take me home.

"But what about my backpack?" I said. "And my bike. They're still at school."

As the nurse had cut my shirt I had to wear the hospital gown home. We stopped by my school and Haakon ran in and got my backpack for me, and my dad picked up my bike and put it in the back of the car. Then my dad dropped me off at home before going back to work.

I took off the hospital gown and put a new shirt on and went into the kitchen. I microwaved a bag of popcorn, and got a can of Coke from the fridge. Then I decided to have a *Pirates of the Caribbean* marathon.

Jack Sparrow sailed into shore while I ate my popcorn with my left hand. It wasn't cooked to perfection but it was pretty darn close. The doctor had told me that I needed to have the sling on for four weeks this time. At least now I couldn't have PE for a while. Then I wondered if Haakon would still fail me for missing his class?

## 20

# It Happened One Day

I think it was a Tuesday. I don't know for sure, which is weird, because I'm usually very good at remembering these things. But I think it was a Tuesday. The day my mom told me that she was going away for a while.

We were sitting in the kitchen and Sigve and my dad were still at work and she said that she was going away on a business trip. I was very surprised because she has never gone on business trips before.

"Where are you going?" I asked.

"To Oslo," she said.

"How long will you be gone?"

"Ninety days."

Ninety days sounded like a very long time for a

business trip and I asked if she really had to stay away for that long.

She said she had to.

I have never been to Oslo and I asked if I could come visit her.

"Of course you can't, you have school."

"But maybe I could come for a weekend."

"No, Malin."

"Why not?"

"Malin, please, you're killing me with all these questions."

I looked at my mom. I wanted to ask her when she was going but I didn't want to kill her.

Then my mom said, "Let's get some ice cream."

She clearly wanted to give me a treat to stop me from asking questions. That made me feel like a five year old. And I sort of liked it.

My mom got out the chocolate-chip ice cream from the freezer and put two scoops in a bowl and gave it to me and I ate it with my left hand. Chocolate-chip is my favourite but for some reason it didn't taste very good.

After the ice cream I felt like getting some fresh air, so I went for a walk. I was crossing the playground at the end of Thorstein Street when I saw a boy sitting on one of the benches, playing with his phone. The boy was Ruben.

He met my eyes and I raised my hand to wave at him, but he didn't wave back. He just looked in a different direction, got up from the bench and walked away. My heart dropped to the bottom of my stomach. I didn't understand why he didn't say hello. I told myself there was a possibility that maybe he didn't see me, but deep down I knew that he had.

I continued across the playground and walked over to Magnus's house. He was in the garage, working on his new moped. I didn't want to talk about my mom or Ruben, so I talked about Hanna instead. I told him that Hanna hadn't replied to my text and I hadn't seen her in school and I didn't know what to do. But Magnus wasn't listening. He said that the rear brake wasn't doing what it should be doing and that he probably needed to replace the brake shoe or something like that.

I said, "Hey, do you want to go inside and watch TV or something?"

"Not now," Magnus said, without looking up from what he was doing. "I am trying to figure this out."

"Fine!" I said. "Stay here and play with your stupid bike." And then I went home.

I was feeling hungry so I went into the kitchen to see if dinner was nearly ready. But it didn't seem like my mom had started on dinner yet. Instead she was standing over the sink and pouring bottles of wine down the drain. Maybe her heart was as good as it could get.

"What's for dinner?" I asked.

My mom turned around. "Oh, hello," she said.

"Hello," I said. "What's for dinner?"

"There is lasagne in the fridge. You can warm it up in the microwave if you like."

After I had eaten I turned the TV on. NRK was showing an old episode of *Bondi Rescue*. That made me think of Ruben and how weird he was when I saw him at the playground. I didn't understand why he had ignored me, because the last time I talked to him everything had seemed fine.

I decided to ask Google. According to one discussion forum, it is not uncommon to meet a boy, hit it off, and then suddenly hear nothing but silence from him. Most people seemed to be pretty certain that this meant he really wasn't that into you. But some people said it could actually mean that he was just really busy, or that he had something on his mind. One girl gave an example of how she hadn't heard anything from a boy she had recently started dating and it turned out that he had had a death in his family and was upset and didn't want to talk to anybody. Apparently it is hard for guys to talk to girls about emotional things, especially when they don't know you that well.

I felt a glimmer of hope and realized that I was smiling. And then I felt guilty for hoping that Ruben had had a death in his family.

# 21

# Late

I woke up to the smell of bacon and I knew straight away that something was up. It wasn't Sunday or my birthday or Easter morning or anything, and still I smelled bacon. It made me feel queasy.

I climbed out of bed and opened my bedroom door. With my eyes adjusting to the light, I went into the kitchen in my pyjamas.

There were two pans on the stove, one with scrambled eggs and one with bacon. And at the kitchen counter my mom was making *lapper* on the big round griddle that used to belong to Grandma. She added small portions of batter to the griddle with a ladle, until it was full of what looked like small thick pancakes. Then she turned around and noticed I was there. She jumped and dropped the ladle on the floor. "Oh, Malin," she said. "You startled me. Sit down, I've made breakfast." She picked up the ladle from the floor and put it in the sink as I sat down at the table.

"What would you like to eat?" she asked. "There's eggs and bacon and I am making *lapper*." She got a spatula from the drawer and starting flipping them over. We have never had *lapper* for breakfast. Ever.

Then I noticed the suitcases. I had a direct view into the hallway from where I was sitting and there they were. There was one small suitcase on top of a big suitcase and my mom's burgundy duffel coat was neatly folded on top of them. That's when I started crying. I wasn't exactly sure why, but I couldn't hold back the tears. They ran silently down my cheeks.

With her back to me, my mom said, "So what would you like for breakfast?" She was using the spatula to put the finished *lapper* on a cooling rack. She turned and looked at me. My bottom lip was trembling and a tear ran off my cheek and continued down my pyjama top.

My mom looked at me for a moment. Then she said, "You can eat in front of the TV if you like."

I wasn't hungry, so I just had a glass of orange juice while watching *Good Morning Norway*. "Are you sure you don't want some *lapper*?" my mom said, but I didn't. I just had another glass of orange juice. Then Sigve came in, wearing his work clothes. He sat down and told me to change the channel. He ate a portion of bacon and eggs and then he had four *lapper* with strawberry jam and sour cream. Afterwards, he went into the kitchen and said something to my mom that I couldn't hear and then he left.

I went into the bathroom and brushed my teeth and got dressed in my room. Then I put the books that I needed for school in my backpack, and put it over my left shoulder.

When I came back to the living room my dad was standing next to the suitcases with the car keys in his hands. He said he was taking my mom to the airport and that he could give me a ride to school if I wanted.

"I want to go to the airport," I said. My dad said I couldn't because the airport is forty minutes away from Haasund and I would be late for school. My eyes filled with tears again and my mom said that I could come to the airport if I wanted.

"No one has died from being late for school once in a while," she said. I wiped my tears away with the back of my hand and put my coat on.

We arrived at the airport at 7.49 a.m. My dad helped my mom take the suitcases inside and then he carried the big suitcase to the baggage drop-off.

I wanted to say goodbye to my mom at the gate but I wasn't allowed to go through security because I didn't have a boarding card.

"We'll say goodbye here," my mom said.

"Please don't leave," I said.

"Don't make this harder than it already is."

My mom's voice was sharp so I didn't say anything else.

And then, in a much milder voice, she said, "I will be back on the twentieth of April. And we can write to each other and talk on the phone. Every day."

I didn't answer.

"I'll wave to you before I go through the security gate," she said. She was treating me like a little child again, but I said okay.

My mom and dad looked awkwardly at each other, and for a brief moment I wondered if they were going to kiss. I have never seen my mom and dad kiss. Then my mom stroked my dad's upper arm a couple of times. Not soft and gentle, but quick and rough, the way you pat a dog.

I stood to one side and watched my mom wait in line for her turn to go through security. My dad kept tapping his foot and checking his watch. When my mom reached the front of the line, I saw her put her handbag and some other things in a box on the conveyer belt before putting the small suitcase through. And then, right before she walked through the security metal detector, she turned and waved at me and I waved back with my left hand.

My dad didn't say much on the way back, but he let me pick the station on the radio. At 9.12 a.m. we arrived at my school and my dad said, "Okay, I will see you this afternoon."

"You have to write me a note," I said.

"What?"

"A note for me to give to my teacher. Explaining why I am late."

"Erm, okay." He opened the glove compartment and found an old receipt for washer fluid. He wrote something on the back of the receipt and gave it to me. It said, *Malin is late today because of an emergency.*

"I think you have to be a bit more specific," I said.

He took the note back and stroked his moustache a couple of times before adding something at the bottom of the note. He handed it to me and I looked at it. He had added the word *situation* at the bottom. *Malin is late today because of an emergency situation.*

Before I went into my classroom I stopped by the toilets to look in the mirror. My eyes were red and it looked like I had been crying. I splashed some water onto my face and rubbed my eyes, but that made it worse. I decided to wait until it didn't look like I had been crying, so I sat down on the floor and played some games on my phone.

At 9.48 I went into my classroom. We were having Social Studies with Harald Foss. Everyone in my class was sitting at their desk, writing. Probably working on a task. I walked up to Harald's desk and gave him the note. He took a quick look at it and then he looked at me. "Who wrote this?"

"My dad did."

He looked at the note again. "Okay," he said, "the class is just about to present their work. Have a seat."

The task Harald had given the class was to write a short piece about someone who inspires you. It didn't have to be a celebrity, it could be a parent or an older sibling or even a teacher.

Most of the girls had written about different top bloggers who make tons of money writing about make-up and fashion. They talked about how inspiring it was that they had a job they loved, flexible hours and earned a living at the same time.

Most of the boys had chosen football players. One had picked Lionel Messi, one Luis Suárez and three Cristiano Ronaldo. Five of them had chosen Martin Ødegaard and all five of them talked about how cool it was that he was a professional football player at such a young age.

I nearly fell asleep.

Then the bell rang and it was time for lunch. I hadn't had anything for breakfast and I was starving. And then I realized that I had forgotten to bring lunch.

I reached into my backpack to get out the change I kept there. I still had the twenty-one kroner that I had been collecting and I decided that I would go across the street to the Coop and buy something to eat.

Then I noticed two people standing next to my desk. It was Frida and Julie.

"Hi," Frida said.

"Hello," I said.

"Are you okay?"

"Yes."

"Are you really?" Julie said. "Because it kind of looks like you have been crying."

"I'm fine."

"Good," Frida said. "And at least you don't have to worry about Ruben bothering you any more. We took care of that for you."

"What do you mean?" I said.

"Well, you know how he was hanging around you all the time, even though you clearly didn't like him?"

"Yeah," Julie said. "You did tell us that you didn't like him."

"And as he obviously couldn't take a hint, we told him to back off," Frida said.

Julie nodded. "We also said that you found him gross and weird. I know you didn't say that, but sometimes you have to exaggerate with guys to make sure they get the message."

I didn't know what to say. My legs felt weak and my palms were sweaty. So this was why Ruben had stopped talking to me.

Frida gasped. "Oh God. You don't actually like him, do you? Because if you do, you shouldn't be going around telling people that you don't. That is really mean."

"Yeah," Julie said. "We were only trying to help you."

I didn't answer. I quickly put the change in my pocket and walked out of the classroom. I had to talk to Ruben.

I saw Ruben in the courtyard, but he was not alone. He was talking to this girl. I don't really know her, but I have seen her around school. She is in the same year as Ruben, one year younger than me, and I think her name is Isabel or Isabella or something. Her hair is long and blonde. And curly. They were both smiling.

When Ruben saw that I was looking at them he gave the girl a nod with his head to signal that they should go in the opposite direction. And then they walked off.

I had to find a way for Ruben to listen to me, but I didn't know how.

I found it hard to concentrate and I realized that I was still really hungry, so I walked to the Coop to get my lunch. I decided to get a two-pack of chocolate buns. They cost nineteen kroner so I couldn't afford a drink, but that was okay.

On my way to the checkout I saw my brother Sigve. I had never seen him at work before. He was standing in the baking section and helping an old lady put bags of flour into her shopping trolley. He was smiling and talking to her in a friendly voice. He was acting like a human being, which was weird.

# 22

## Countdown

My dad said that I wasn't allowed to call my mom for twenty-four hours. I asked why and he said she needed time to settle in. I asked why that takes exactly twenty-four hours and he told me to stop asking stupid questions and just accept that I couldn't call her yet.

I said goodbye to my mom at 7.52 a.m., so that meant that I could call her at 7.52 a.m. before I went into school the next day.

"It doesn't work that way," my dad said.

"How does it work then?"

"She checked in at 4 p.m. so you can call her from 4 p.m. tomorrow."

"What do you mean by 'checked in'?"

My dad looked at me, but he didn't say anything.

"Do you mean at the hotel?"

"Right. Exactly."

"But how can it take so long to settle in at a hotel?"

"Because…" My dad paused. "She has meetings and stuff. Business meetings."

"But…"

Then my dad sighed and told me to go and watch TV or something.

But I didn't want to watch TV. I went up to my room and got out a pencil and a blank sheet of paper. If Ruben didn't want to talk to me then maybe I could send him a letter. That way he would have to listen to what I wanted to say.

I had never written a letter to a boy before and I wasn't sure what to write. I started the letter with *Dear Ruben*. That was the easy part. Then I wrote that I didn't find him weird and gross. Then I erased that, because it sounded silly. So I wrote that I liked him. Now the letter said, *Dear Ruben, I like you*. It sounded stupid and juvenile.

I decided that writing Ruben a letter was a bad idea so I crumpled the letter into a ball and threw it in the bin. Then I regretted throwing it away and I took it out of the bin and tried to straighten it the best I could.

I looked at my watch. It showed the time was 4.48 p.m.

That meant that it was twenty-three hours and twelve minutes until I could call my mom.

At 5.16 p.m. my dad called my name and said dinner was ready. I put the letter away and went into the kitchen. We were having frozen pizza, which doesn't usually happen on a Thursday. And we didn't eat together at the table. Sigve had his pizza down in the basement, my dad ate in front of the TV, and I ate in the kitchen while reading a science magazine I found on the counter. There was an article saying that the Earth now had two moons.

NASA had discovered a mini-moon orbiting the earth. It was found by an asteroid survey telescope in Hawaii and named *2016 HO3*. The article said it was likely that the second moon had existed for a long time, but no one knew about it until now.

I looked at the clock above the door. It was 5.23 p.m. Twenty-two hours and thirty-seven minutes to go.

After dinner, Sigve rushed out the door to get to his evening shift at Coop. My dad didn't ask me if I had finished my homework yet. But that's not really something my mom would do either.

At 6.43 p.m. my dad turned off the TV and went into his study to do some work. The house was silent, which was weird, because my dad is usually the one who yells and he was still at home.

I took the magazine into the living room. I turned the TV back on and left it on TV3, which was showing *The King of Queens* reruns. I let it play in the background while I read the magazine.

At 10.02 p.m. I went to bed. I took the magazine with me and read about Neanderthals and the great white shark and mummies. I completely lost track of time and suddenly I was feeling really sleepy. I put the magazine away and turned off my bedside lamp and closed my eyes. Then I realized that I had forgotten to do my homework.

I went out into the hallway and got my backpack and took it into the kitchen. The lights were off everywhere so I figured my dad had gone to bed already.

The sink was full of dirty dishes and there was leftover pizza on the counter. I sat down at the table and solved the four maths problems that I had for homework. If I put the notebook in my lap diagonally, I could still manage to write with my right hand even though it was in the sling. But if I did it for too long my arm started to hurt and then I had to switch to my left hand.

I did my English homework, which was to fill in the blanks in some sentences by inserting words in the correct tense. That was pretty easy. I don't know the rules, but I know which are correct from remembering how people speak on television. The next subject I had to do was history.

I had to read a chapter about the population growth in Europe from 1850 to 1930, and answer some questions on a sheet. But I was too tired to read. I knew a lot about the Neanderthals and the great white shark, but nothing about people in Europe. I decided to leave the answers blank. Maybe I'd have time to read the chapter the next morning before school?

As I put the history book back in my backpack I noticed a crumpled piece of paper at the bottom. I pulled it out and unfolded it. It was my assignment, *What would you do if you got to be God for one day?* The one I failed. I was supposed to write a new one, but then I fell off my bike and missed a day of school and forgot all about it. My teacher, Trude Fjell, hadn't asked me about it either. I put the paper inside my history book and decided to write a new one later.

The clock above the door was ticking loudly. It showed the time was 11.39 p.m. It was sixteen hours and twenty-one minutes until I could call my mom.

Sometimes it was hard to fall asleep with my arm in the sling. It felt tight and I was not able to lie on my right side. I lay awake for hours listening to the rain pouring down outside.

* * *

I didn't get a chance to read my history homework the next morning.

I was really tired and I was just barely able to get out of bed when my alarm clock rang. But the questions had multiple-choice answers, so I circled some at random while eating breakfast.

Hanna wasn't at school so I figured she was sick again. I couldn't know for sure because I hadn't talked to her in seven days and twenty-two hours.

At the end of fourth period I handed in my history homework and hoped for the best.

I got home at 2.24 p.m. I watched a couple of episodes of *Glee* to keep busy while waiting to call Mom. I thought it might help to pass the time, but it didn't. I missed most of what was happening and kept staring at my watch.

At 4 p.m. sharp I called my mom's mobile, but it was switched off. I didn't have any other number I could reach her on, and my dad wouldn't be home for at least thirty-four minutes.

I felt angry because my dad had said that I could call her at 4 p.m. that day, and now I couldn't. My dad was a liar.

I did my homework. I drank chocolate milk and ate pretzel sticks. I watched *The Ranch* and I didn't laugh once.

At 5.28 p.m. my dad came home from work. He put

down his laptop bag next to the front door and kicked his shoes off. Then he took his coat off and put it away before sitting down in his armchair.

"Liar," I said and went into my room.

I lay in bed and stared at the ceiling. My dad was a liar and my mom was stupid because she could have called me at 4 p.m. and she didn't.

At 5.45 p.m. my dad came into my room and held his mobile phone out to me. He said that my mom was on the phone and asked me if I wanted to talk to her. I told him that I didn't want to talk to anyone and he left my room. I waited two whole minutes before running in and telling him that I wanted to talk to her after all.

"Hello?" I said.

"Hello," my mom said. "How are you?"

"Fine."

"How's school?"

"Fine," I said. "How's Oslo?"

"It's good."

"How were your meetings?"

"Meetings?"

Then I heard someone talking in the background.

"I have to go," my mom said.

"But..."

"I will talk to you soon, okay?"

I didn't get a chance to answer because she hung up and all I could hear was the dial tone.

I got the science magazine and read about Alexander Graham Bell and how he didn't invent the telephone after all. Some guy named Antonio Meucci did. Alexander Graham Bell was a liar too. In 1880 the first telephone network was installed in Norway. Shortly after, local telephone companies were created in several municipalities around the country. I thought about those first phone calls people around here made. I bet they only talked to people who lived too far away to visit. And I bet they had a lot to talk about.

At 6.19 p.m. I put the magazine away and washed up for dinner. And for dinner we had pizza again.

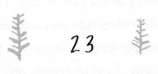

# 23

# Death

A couple of days ago a sixteen-year-old boy crashed his moped on Gustav Street. The roads were still a bit wet after the rain and the police think that's what caused the accident. The boy lost control of the vehicle and drove right off the road and into some huge rocks. He died instantly.

The boy was Magnus Helvik. The boy was my cousin. Magnus is dead and he wasn't old and he wasn't sick. He was just here one day and the next day he wasn't.

I hope that when it's my time to go I see it coming. That I die from a fatal disease where the doctor says, "You've got six months to live." That way I'll have some time to prepare. I'd burn my diary and that letter that I wrote to Ruben Oftedal but never sent. I'd also get rid of that box in the back of my closet. The one with the two cigarettes, and the article that explains how to kiss a boy. And then I'd probably throw away my bright pink Barbie underwear as well. Just to make sure that I'm not accidentally wearing them the day I go.

Magnus saved my life in a pool once. I am sorry I couldn't save his. But how could I?

I couldn't wrap my head around the fact that Magnus was gone for ever. I wasn't going to see him again. He wasn't coming back.

Then I learned that my mom wasn't coming home for Magnus's funeral.

I was talking to her on the phone and she told me that she wouldn't make it back.

"But you have to," I said. "He's your nephew."

"Malin, that's a terrible thing to say, I would be there if I could."

And then she told me that I needed to take care of something for her. "In the blue vase, on the Normann Copenhagen side table, there is some money. I want you to buy a tin of biscuits from Holberg's shop and take them over to Aunt Lillian."

"Okay," I said.

Then her voice sounded distant and hollow. "Of course,

store-bought biscuits are rather terrible in this situation. No grieving mother should receive store-bought biscuits."

Then she went silent.

"Mom?"

"Oh, you'll need to get flowers too," she said. "Go down to Margot's Flowers and ask for a condolences bouquet with lilies. She will know what that means."

After I hung up I went into the living room and looked in the blue vase. There were three one-hundred-kroner notes in there, one two-hundred-kroner note and a bunch of coins. I had never bought flowers before and my mom hadn't told me how much I needed so, just to be safe, I took it all and put it in my backpack.

My mom sounded sad that Aunt Lillian had to get biscuits from Holberg's and that made me feel bad. I didn't know how to make biscuits, but I have made waffles with my mom a couple of times and I thought Aunt Lillian might appreciate some home-made waffles instead.

The kitchen was very messy. In the sink was a tower of dirty dishes and the kitchen counter was covered in pots and pans and glasses. There wasn't much room to bake, but I managed to find an empty space for the mixing bowl.

The recipe said that the first thing I needed to do was to mix egg and sugar together so I did that and then I put in the milk. It didn't looked half bad until I added the flour.

Then the batter quickly became lumpy and weird and not smooth like it was when I made it with my mom.

I figured the problem might be that I didn't mix the egg and sugar together properly before putting in the milk and flour, so I decided to start over. I got a new bowl and cracked two new eggs and put the sugar in. But when I added the flour the same thing happened again.

I figured the reason I couldn't get the batter right was because I wasn't able to mix it properly using my left hand. I needed more power. So I decided to get the mixer out of the cupboard. There wasn't a lot of room left on the kitchen counter but I managed to squeeze it on. I cracked the last two eggs into the bowl and put more sugar in.

I put the mixer on full speed and went over to the table and started measuring the flour and baking powder. After a couple of seconds I noticed that the mixer was moving, probably due to the full speed. It moved closer and closer to the edge of the counter. I hurried over to save it – but I was too late and the mixer crashed to the floor, the bowl flew across the room and the batter spilled everywhere.

Then my dad walked into the kitchen. "What the hell is going on?"

I looked at the mess I had made. There was batter all over the floor and it had splattered on the drawers of the kitchen counter and on the fridge. I looked at my dad.

"No grieving mother should receive store-bought biscuits," I whispered.

My dad looked at me. "Okay," he said.

My dad helped me clean up the mess. We mopped the floor and threw out all the lumpy batter that was left in the mixing bowls. We unloaded the dishwasher and then we reloaded it and then we wiped down the kitchen counter.

When we were done there were still traces of flour on the kitchen counter and some batter running down the fridge, but I didn't care. I sat down at the table. My dad was just standing in the middle of the room, staring out the window. But it was an empty stare. Like he wasn't focusing on anything.

"Dad?"

He blinked a few times and rubbed his eyes before looking at me. "Yes?" he said.

"Do you know how to make waffles?" I asked.

"No, I don't."

"Biscuits?"

"Afraid not."

"Oh."

My dad looked out the window again and stroked his moustache a couple of times.

"Maybe we could get someone to help us?" he said. "Who do we know that bakes?"

I thought for a moment. Then I said, "Aunt Lillian."

My dad laughed, and that made me laugh too.

Across the road from us, in number seventeen, there lives an old widow with no children, named Ågot Ueland. My dad said that women like her would die to have someone to bake for. So he went over and asked if she could help us. Apparently he was right, because a couple of hours later she came over with a basket full of baked goods.

"I made some cinnamon rolls," she said, "and then I made some muffins in case she doesn't like cinnamon rolls. And then, just in case she doesn't like muffins, I made oatmeal cookies too." She looked at me with eyes that smiled even though her mouth didn't. Her grey hair was all out of order and she had millions of tiny wrinkles at the corners of her eyes.

"Of course I forgot to ask if your aunt has any allergies. If that is the case I can go home and make something else."

I said it was okay and thanked her. Ågot looked slightly disappointed and said, "Well, let me know if you need anything else." Then she went back to her house.

I looked at the basket and wondered if it was all just a waste, because I've read somewhere that losing a loved one also makes you lose your appetite. Nevertheless I picked up the basket and headed over to Knuds Street so

I could give it to Aunt Lillian. It felt like I had a thousand bricks in my stomach and I didn't really want to go.

If I got to be God for one day I'd change things around so that Magnus didn't crash his moped on Gustav Street. In fact, I'd change things so he didn't drive his moped at all that day. He just ate dinner, did his homework and then watched TV with his mom. And nothing else happened.

I know it's selfish. I know it's not allowed. I'm just saying. Who wouldn't?

## 24

# Where Magnus Used to Live

According to Google Maps, Knuds Street is a ten-minute walk from my house. I normally walk it in somewhere between eight minutes and fifty-eight seconds and nine minutes and forty-three seconds. The basket was heavy to carry with only one hand, so I had to stop and take quite a few breaks. That was okay, because I wasn't really eager to arrive. Even though I took my time and walked slower than I ever had, it only took fifteen minutes and nineteen seconds before I stood outside Magnus's house. What used to be Magnus's house.

I rang the doorbell and waited for Aunt Lillian to answer the door. I realized that I didn't know what to say to her. Was I supposed to say *kondolerer*? When I was eleven, my grandma died and a lot of people came to our house to give us flowers and drink tea. After a visit from some of our neighbours, I heard my mom tell my dad that she hated that word. "*Kondolerer* is a terrible word," she said. I didn't really understand why, because all it means is that you are sorry that someone died: "my condolences".

Then Aunt Lillian opened the door. Her eyes were sore and red and her hair was in a bun on top of her head. And even though it was only a couple of days since Magnus crashed his bike, she already looked thinner.

"Oh, hey, Malin." When she smiled she looked even more tired. "What a nice surprise."

"I brought baked goods," I said.

I guess the polite thing to do when someone shows up on your doorstep with a basket of baked goods is to invite them in. And I suppose the polite thing to do when someone invites you in is to accept.

As we walked through the living room I noticed that there were flowers everywhere. They were on every side table, shelf and everywhere else one could think to put bouquets of flowers. Carnations, white roses and lilies. And those white ones with the long petals with the yellow centre.

It looked like a flower shop in there. It smelled like one too. That's when I realized that I forgot to buy flowers.

Aunt Lillian led the way to the kitchen, where the table was also covered with bouquets of more roses and more lilies and more carnations. I didn't know where to put the basket and Aunt Lillian took it from me and put it on the counter. "Oh my," she said. "Did you make all these?"

"No," I said. "The widow down the street did. Old widows would die to have someone to bake for."

"Oh," Aunt Lillian said. And I immediately regretted saying the word "die".

Aunt Lillian put the kettle on and I helped her put the cinnamon rolls, the muffins and the cookies on a glass tray. I brought plates and teacups into the living room and Aunt Lillian moved some flower arrangements to the side to make room on the table. Then we sat down.

Aunt Lillian took a cookie from the tray and immediately took a bite of it. She chewed it slowly and closed her eyes, like she was taking in the taste. "It's been years since I last had a good oatmeal cookie," she said and put the rest of it in her mouth. Still chewing, she helped herself to another one.

She pushed the tray closer to me and gave me a nod to encourage me to help myself. I put a cinnamon roll on my plate even though I wasn't hungry. I looked at the photos on the wall. Aunt Lillian holding Magnus on the day of his baptism. Magnus on his confirmation day. Magnus with a gold medal around his neck, which he was holding up to show to the camera. A thought popped into my head that there wouldn't be one of him on his wedding day. I pushed the cinnamon roll around on my plate. A part of me kept thinking that, at any minute, Magnus would pop around the corner with his goofy smile and say a corny line. At the same time, I knew that he wouldn't.

Aunt Lillian finished the cookie and helped herself to a muffin. "When Magnus was a little boy he wanted to become a surgeon. Did you know that?" She laughed. "He was such a klutz as a child – I wouldn't trust him with a plastic fork, much less a scalpel." Then she said quietly, "But when he started swimming he found his real talent." She broke off a piece of the muffin and put it in her mouth before continuing. "Magnus and I had a lot of disagreements for a while. We were bickering a lot. About small things, that didn't matter. But when Magnus took his bike out that day, the last thing I said to him was that I loved him. I am very thankful that our last conversation ended on a good note."

The last thing I said to Magnus was to play with his stupid bike. And that is what he did. I kept pushing the cinnamon roll around on my plate, because I didn't know what to do with it.

"This was nobody's fault," Aunt Lillian said. "It's just

one of those awful, awful things that happens."

"I forgot to bring flowers," I said.

"Thank God." Aunt Lillian laughed. "I am running out of room."

"I was supposed to bring flowers."

She smiled her tired smile again. "It's okay, Malin."

I came there to be a comfort to Aunt Lillian. But she was the one comforting me. Then Aunt Lillian pointed at the roll on my plate and said, "Don't worry about it. I'll have it if you don't want it."

On my way out I noticed a bunch of photographs on the old wooden desk in the hallway. "What's this?" I said.

"Oh, I was just looking through some old photos," Aunt Lillian said.

I had a quick glance through them. There was a photo of Magnus as a little boy on a kick scooter, with a Mickey Mouse plaster on his knee. Another was of Magnus on his first day of school, grinning at the camera, his front teeth missing. There were also some pictures of me and Sigve and my mom and dad. Then there was a photo of a baby boy who I didn't recognize, sitting in a high chair. He had food all over his face and a head full of brown curls.

"Who is this?" I asked.

"Why, that is Magnus."

Magnus? He looked nothing like the Magnus I knew.

Aunt Lillian picked up the photo and smiled. "He lost all those wonderful curls before he turned two."

It was already dark when I walked home. The air was crisp and when I breathed, smoke came out of my mouth. As I walked down Trysil Street I opened up my coat and took my woollen hat off. I wanted to be cold.

# 25

# Open Doors and Broken Bridges

This morning I stayed under the covers and listened to my dad roam around in the kitchen. I heard cupboards being opened and shut and the sound of cutlery and glass clinking together. He was making a lot of racket for someone who normally doesn't eat breakfast. Maybe he was looking for the coffee. Then I heard him leave through the front door. One hour and eleven minutes later, I heard Sigve leave as well. Then I got out of bed.

I had decided that I wasn't going to school. My mom was away, Hanna wasn't speaking to me. And Magnus was gone. So I didn't want to go to school and I figured my dad wouldn't notice if I stayed at home anyway.

I got up and brushed my teeth but I didn't get dressed.

I let Oscar in and fed him. I got out the science magazine and made myself a sandwich with strawberry jam. Then I sat down at the kitchen table and flipped through the magazine, but I had already read all the articles.

After breakfast I went down to the basement and turned the Xbox on. Sigve had got a new game. I think the point of it was to shoot as many people as possible, so I did. I shot people in the head. In the chest. In the back. I shot a guy's face off and watched the blood pulsate out of his neck before he fell to the ground. Then I felt sick to my stomach and turned the Xbox off.

I wondered what Magnus thought about in the moment of the accident. Did he know that he was going to die? The police said that he didn't. They said that he died instantly and that he didn't feel any pain. But how could they know?

I didn't want to think about death any more so I turned the TV on. Animal Planet was showing a documentary about elephants. The narrator said that elephants mostly sleep standing up. Sometimes they lie down, but usually not for more than an hour, because they are so heavy that if they lie down for longer they risk crushing their internal organs.

I remember reading somewhere that elephants mourn the death of fellow elephants. If they stumble upon another elephant's remains, they lift up its bones with their trunks, balance them on their tusks and put them in their mouth, as if they are trying to determine if they belong to someone they know. Some elephants have been observed standing over an elephant's corpse for several days, not wanting to leave their side. Apparently there have also been observations of elephants shedding tears over the loss of a loved one.

Even elephants cry when they lose a family member. So why hadn't I been able to cry about Magnus yet? Was I a bad person? I had to be. Even animals had more heart than me.

When you're all alone in a big house it can make you think a lot. So I decided to go to school after all. I just couldn't be alone with my thoughts any more. I let Oscar out, got dressed and packed my bag. Then I walked to school.

When I walked in through the main door of Haasund Lower Secondary School I noticed straight away that something was going on. A bunch of kids were standing in line outside Principal Skogen's office.

I overheard two girls talking about what had happened. Apparently someone had carved the word *whore* into someone's desk. Even before I heard, I immediately knew who the desk belonged to. In Haasund a young girl can have sex a thousand times without anyone giving it any thought. But if she becomes pregnant she automatically becomes a whore.

I walked down the halls to get to class. I hadn't seen Hanna around school in a while and I hadn't talked to her in thirteen days, twenty-three hours and twelve minutes. She didn't even know about my mom.

But today she had showed up to do a test. At least that is what she told me when I ran into her on my way to class.

I came around the corner and there she was.

"Hey," she said.

"Hey," I said.

"You hurt your arm again."

"Yes."

"That sucks."

"Yes."

"I'm going home now. I just came in to do a test."

"Okay."

She paused. Then she said, "So, I heard. About your cousin, I mean. I heard."

"Oh," I said.

"I know how it feels. My grandfather died when I was a child and I loved him very much."

I had lost two grandparents. It wasn't the same. They were old and sick. It was sad, but it wasn't the same.

"So, yeah, I know how you feel."

She didn't. She thought she knew everything just because she was sixteen. And pregnant. She wasn't an adult. Just because she had a boyfriend and was pregnant, it didn't mean she knew everything.

"Whore!" I said, and walked away.

At 10.28 a.m. I entered my classroom and the squeaky door made everyone turn their heads to look at me. This was the second time I had been late for class. Ever. My teacher, Trude Fjell, who was standing in front of the class, turned and looked at me through her red glasses that are just a tiny bit too big for her face.

"Hi, Malin," Trude said.

"Hello."

"Do you have a note for me?"

"No."

"Oh. Did you leave it at home?"

"No."

She looked at me for a little while before she said, "Okay. Please, take a seat. We were just about to start with some grammar."

I sat down at my desk and opened my book to page 136, because that was what Trude had written on the whiteboard. First we were going to do some repetition exercises and conjugate a few verbs. This is really simple because there is only one right answer.

Just as I was about to start, Trude came over to my desk. She bent down and whispered, "Don't worry about being late. I will let it slide this one time. I know things are not easy these days, with your cousin and all."

She looked at me as if she wanted me to say something, but I didn't know what to say because she hadn't asked me a question or anything.

So I just said, "Okay."

She smiled. "And my door is always open if you need to talk."

She wasn't talking about a real door, it is just an expression. Trude doesn't have an office or anything. She has a desk in the teacher's lounge upstairs, but that door is always closed.

"Okay," I said again.

I started to fill in the verbs in the different tenses. It was, as expected, quite simple, so I did the first couple of exercises really fast. For the next task we had to write down some examples of what is typical for Norwegian grammar and compare it to how it is done in English. This required a bit more thinking, but it still wasn't hard.

When the bell rang for lunch break I lost focus and looked up from my book. Magnus used to say that it was impossible to get my attention when I had my face in a book. I looked at my watch and realized that I hadn't thought about him in twenty-seven minutes and forty-three seconds. It was good to have something to focus on. I decided not to miss any more school from now on. I took my time packing my things, while thinking about how to spend the next half-hour. My classmates left the room one by one as I neatly put my pencil and eraser in my pencil case.

I went out to the corridor, but I didn't know what to do, because I wasn't hungry and I didn't feel like reading. I looked at my watch. It showed the time was 11.09 a.m. I clicked on the stopwatch function. I noticed that it still had Magnus's record stored. Four minutes and forty-six seconds. Magnus was gone but his record was still there. And now it would stay like that for ever.

I had a really good stopwatch, but nothing to time. I started to play around with it by starting and stopping the timer at random. I made sure to stop it in time so that it didn't erase the record. Then I decided to check how long it took before someone wearing a blue sweater walked by. It took two minutes and forty-five seconds. Then I decided to check how long it took before someone with a green sweater walked by. I didn't find out though, because I was interrupted. By Frida.

So I stopped the timer.

"Hey," Frida said.

"Hello," I said.

"Listen, I just wanted to say that I am sorry about telling Ruben that you don't like him."

I didn't answer.

"I really was just trying to help you."

I reset the timer on my watch and looked around to see if anyone in a green sweater was walking by.

"What are you doing anyway?" Frida said.

"I am timing how long it takes before someone in a green sweater walks by."

"What? Why?"

"Because I like to know how long things take."

"Okay?"

"I have to make sure it doesn't go past four minutes and forty-six seconds though. Or else it will erase my cousin Magnus's record."

"Oh, right. I heard about your cousin. I'm sorry."

"Thanks."

Frida pointed at my watch. "What's that thing you said about a record?"

"I used to help Magnus time how long he could hold his breath underwater. His personal best of four minutes and forty-six seconds is stored in my watch. If I time anything longer than that it will disappear."

She nodded. "Well, I have to go. Have fun with whatever you are doing."

Then she walked away. Just before she was about to disappear around the corner, she turned back. "Oh, by the way…" She smiled. "I like your watch."

# 26

## Goodbye

The night before Magnus's funeral I stood out on the porch in the rain without my coat on. I figured if I got really sick, I wouldn't have to go to the funeral. The thought of Magnus lying in a coffin and putting him into the ground made me feel sick.

But the morning of the funeral, I woke up and I felt fine. My mom always said that if I didn't wear a coat when it rained I would get sick. Apparently this was another lie.

It was a Wednesday and even though I had the day off from school I woke up at 6.44 a.m. My stomach was in a knot and I felt nervous and I just couldn't sleep any more. So I got up.

I had talked to my mom on the phone the night before,

and she'd suggested that I should put on the dark grey dress that I'd worn last Christmas. I didn't really want to wear it, because it is itchy. But when I looked through my closet, it was the only one that seemed appropriate. I lay the dress and a pair of black leggings on my bed. Then I went into the bathroom and brushed my teeth.

When I walked into the living room all the lights were off, and the house was completely quiet. I left the lights as they were and turned on the TV. The only shows on were ones that sold strange fitness products that I had never heard about and cartoons for little children. And *Dr. Phil*.

There was a man on the *Dr. Phil* show who had been accused of murdering his wife, and he agreed to take a lie detector test to prove his innocence. Dr. Phil said that the results revealed deception. Which meant that the man was lying.

A lie detector test is not 100% accurate. A lot of things can affect the results. Being nervous, high blood pressure and muscular movements are all things that can make it seem like you are lying – even if you are telling the truth. The Integrated Zone Comparison Technique is supposedly one of the best testing formats and has an accuracy of 99.4%. But that is still not 100%.

I turned off the TV and sat in the dark and listened to the silence. I wished that I could tell when people were lying. That, just by looking at them, I could be 100% certain if they were lying or telling the truth. Or maybe I just wished that I was a better liar myself.

Then the lights suddenly came on, which made me jump. It was my dad and when he noticed me he jumped too and said, "What the hell are you doing sitting here in the dark?"

Sigve didn't get up until 8.29 a.m. His hair was all over the place, but it still looked okay. I don't know how he does it. My dad said that we should eat breakfast so we went into the kitchen. But none of us were really hungry. My dad had a cup of coffee and I had a glass of orange juice and Sigve had cereal, but he didn't eat much. He just circled the spoon around and around in his bowl until the little oatmeal squares were all wet and soggy.

Afterwards, I put on my dress and my dad and Sigve put on their dark suits. Then we were ready to go. We picked up Aunt Lillian on our way and we were the first ones who arrived at the church.

The casket was already in place at the end of the aisle. I knew Magnus was in there. But a part of me couldn't believe it. It didn't seem real. On top of the casket and around it were a lot of flowers. All of them had greetings on them. *Hvil i fred* (rest in peace). *En siste hilsen* (one last goodbye). One said, *Høyt elsket, dypt savnet* (dearly loved, deeply missed), and had my and my family's names on it. Then I didn't want to read any more.

Aunt Lillian and my dad went up to the altar to talk to the priest, while Sigve played on his phone. I went around the church and tried all the different benches to see which one was the best. I didn't really need to know if one was better than the others, but it kept my mind occupied.

Twelve minutes and sixteen seconds before the service started, we all sat down in the front row. My dad handed me an "order of service", which had a picture of Magnus on it. It also had his name and date of birth. And date of death. The church started filling up pretty quickly. I saw some of Magnus's friends, and his classmates, and some of the teachers from my school, and a lot of other people who I didn't know. I also saw some of Sigve's friends coming in. I didn't even look for Hanna, because I knew she wouldn't be there. Why would she? I thought about how I probably should apologize to her, but I didn't know if it would matter.

When I was a child I had a snow globe that Grandma and Grandpa bought me in Prague. Inside was a miniature model of the Charles Bridge. And when you shook it fake snow came down and covered the bridge. It was the most beautiful thing I had ever seen. One time, I was playing with some of Sigve's Lego models when he was out and accidentally broke one of them. When Sigve found out, he stormed into my room and yelled and smashed the globe on the floor. Later my mom made him apologize to me, but it didn't really matter. The globe was still broken. And when I apologized to Frida for cutting her hair, it didn't make her hair grow back. But Frida was still very pretty, even with shorter hair. Maybe that's why she decided to forgive me. I called Hanna a whore. And even if I apologized I would still have called her a whore. It couldn't be undone.

The organist started playing and we sang a couple of songs from the order of service. The others did anyway; I just looked at the lyrics. A lot of people were already crying, but not me. I couldn't.

The priest started talking and he said a lot of nice things about Magnus. How he always stood up for his friends, and that he was kind and had a lot of love to give, and that he always put other people's needs above his own. I didn't know how the priest knew these things, but they were all true.

When it was time to carry Magnus out to his final resting place, as I'd heard my dad call it earlier, everyone got up from their seats. The priest walked down the aisle and we followed him. My dad and Sigve and Aunt Lillian and two men who I hadn't met before – third cousins apparently – carried the casket. A couple of days before, Aunt Lillian had said to me that if it wasn't for my sling I could have helped carry it too. I'd just smiled, because I really didn't want to carry the casket. I'd be worried that I'd slip and fall or do something wrong. Having your arm in a sling is very annoying, but it does come in handy sometimes.

We walked out to the graveyard and they put the casket down next to a hole in the ground that was going to be Magnus's grave. We waited until everyone had gathered around in a half circle. It took a long time because there were so many people. My dad put his arm around Aunt Lillian and she turned and sobbed into his chest. I looked up at Sigve. His eyes were red and watery and his shoulders were shaking. I couldn't remember the last time I had seen him cry. It made him look soft and mellow. And kind.

"What the hell are you looking at?" he hissed at me.

Those of us who were Magnus's closest family each put a rose on the casket. When it was my turn, I stepped up and put the flower on the lid and whispered, "Goodbye."

After that, the priest put three handfuls of dirt on the casket as he said, "*Av jord er du kommet, til jord skal du bli, av jord skal du atter oppstå.*"

Then they lowered the casket into the hole in the ground where Magnus was going to stay for ever. And everyone but me sang another song.

* * *

When I went to bed that night I was glad that I did go to the funeral after all. It wasn't as bad as I had imagined and it felt good to hear the priest say all the nice things about Magnus. And to say goodbye to him.

The next morning I woke up with a cold.

## 27

# Back in the Water

Twenty-first of February was my mom's birthday. It was also the day I got my sling off. Which also meant that I had to have PE again. For the rest of the semester we were having swimming class instead though. Swimming is better than PE. There is no ball. But I hadn't been to the pool since my near-death experience, so I was a bit nervous.

Our locker room has three benches for us to put our stuff on. I took my time getting undressed. All the other girls were already in their swimming costumes and on their way to the showers.

Most of the girls in my class don't bother with taking a proper shower. They just quickly get in with their swimming costumes on. As I put my towel around me I could hear the water running in the other room and all the girls laughing and talking. I folded all my clothes and put them in a neat stack on the bench. Lastly I took off my wristwatch and put it on top of my clothes. It showed the time was 12.57.31. I had two minutes and twenty-nine seconds before class started. When I finally entered the shower, all the other girls had already gone upstairs to the pool. I put my towel on the hook on the wall and went in. I pushed the button and quickly soaped myself before rinsing off. Then I put on my swimming costume and my swimming cap and ran up to the pool.

When I got upstairs my whole class were sitting on the benches next to the pool. Boys on one bench and girls on the other. No one tells us to sit like this, but we always do. In front, our teacher, Haakon Krag, was taking attendance. I sat down in the only free seat, closing the gap between the boys and the girls.

Haakon explained that we would start by doing laps back and forth as a warm-up. Then he blew his whistle and everyone jumped in the pool. Except me, I used the ladder. I stayed in the far left lane so that I could grab hold of the edge if I felt the need to. If something happened this time, Magnus wouldn't be there to save me. After fifteen minutes, Haakon blew his whistle and announced that it was time to play a game. Water polo.

We got out of the pool and sat on the benches again, while Haakon quickly went over the rules. He said that water polo was kind of a mix between swimming, football, basketball, handball, ice hockey, rugby and wrestling. Then he said a lot of other things that I immediately forgot about, but basically we were going to shoot a ball into the other team's goal.

Even in swimming class, Haakon mananged to find a way for us to play with a ball.

Haakon split us into two teams and told us to get back into the pool. My plan was to just swim back and forth and try to keep out of the way. But the ball kept bouncing over in my direction.

I was scared I'd injure my shoulder again, so every time the ball came near me I just gently pushed it away with both my hands so someone else could take it.

When Haakon blew his whistle again, my team had lost 11–2. Haakon told us to hit the showers and everyone hurried to the locker rooms.

We have to shower after swimming class too, but all the other girls just hurried into the locker room. I took my swimming costume off, went into the shower and turned on the water. It is the rule.

By the time I got out of the shower, all the other girls had left. I felt straight away that something wasn't right, but I couldn't tell what it was. And then, when I went to get my clothes, I saw it. My watch. It was gone. My blue and white OTS watch that I had put on top of my clothes wasn't there any more. I quickly started searching for it and I ended up throwing all my clothes on the floor. Then I started going through my bag, but I knew that I wouldn't find it. My watch wasn't there. It was gone.

Someone had taken it.

I don't really remember getting dressed. My thoughts were all over the place and I wasn't feeling well. Someone had my watch. Someone had Magnus's record. I know that somehow I collected my things and got dressed because I remember running into Hanna as I crossed the schoolyard. I didn't really run into her, I just saw her. And she saw me too. And she showed me her middle finger before she turned and walked the other way.

Later I talked to my mom on the phone. I don't really know what she said, because I was distracted and thinking of my watch and found it hard to concentrate. All day I kept checking my wrist to see what time it was, even though my watch wasn't there any more. Then my mom said she had to go and we hung up. And then I realized that I had forgotten to wish her a happy birthday.

That night I struggled to fall asleep. I had been looking forward to going to bed because it is much more comfortable without the sling on, and I don't have to worry about which side to sleep on. But even though the sling was off I couldn't sleep, because I was thinking about my watch. Someone had to have taken it. Was it Hanna? She was definitely still mad at me – her giving me the finger confirmed that – but how would she know that I was having swimming class at that point? Could it have been Frida? She had said that she had forgiven me, so why would she suddenly steal my watch? I supposed that any of the other girls could have taken it, but I hadn't done anything to them and I didn't understand why they would do that.

Then I heard Oscar meowing outside my window. I tried to ignore him because I didn't feel like getting out of bed, but he always seems to know when I'm in my room and he doesn't give up easily. So I got up and opened the window so he could jump in. Then I went back to bed and Oscar curled up next to me and within seconds he was asleep. No matter what is going on Oscar is always able to fall asleep straight away.

After a long time I slowly drifted into sleep too. I dreamed that my mom was home; that I lay in bed and could hear my dad's voice speaking calmly and my mom laughing – that cheerful laughter that she only lets out when she is really happy and that I hadn't heard in a long time. Then I woke up and thought about going into the living room to check if she was actually there. But I was really tired and I knew that it was only a dream so I went back to sleep.

# 28

# Watch

The next morning I woke up and checked the time on my phone. What used to be Magnus's phone. It was 6.21 a.m. Lately I had been waking up before the alarm went off a lot. I couldn't see Oscar anywhere so I guess he had left through the window. I went into the bathroom and turned the water on and brushed my teeth. For a brief moment I thought I heard my mom's laughter again. I turned the tap off and listened, but there was nothing. I went back to my room and got dressed. I put on a pair of jeans and my red zip-up hoodie. Then I put my phone in the pocket of my jeans so I could easily check the time. It wasn't the same though. I liked checking the time on my wrist. And I didn't like the thought of someone else having my watch.

I wondered if whoever had it was messing with the stopwatch. And if Magnus's record was still intact. I had to get it back. But how could I get it back, when I didn't even know where it was?

When I walked into the living room I could hear my dad talking to someone in the kitchen. I went in there and saw that he was talking to Aunt Lillian. I was a bit surprised, because it was really early for visitors.

"Oh, hey, Malin," Aunt Lillian said.

"Hello," I said.

Then my dad said that he was late for work and got his things together and left.

"Let me make you some scrambled eggs," Aunt Lillian said. There were some dirty pots and pans on the stove, which Aunt Lillian moved out of the way. She couldn't put them in the sink because that was full of dirty dishes and pans as well. She got a new pan out and started making the eggs. With her back to me, she said, "So, how are you this morning?"

"Not very good."

"What?"

"Not good."

Aunt Lillian moved the pan to one side and came and sat down next to me. Then she put her hand on my arm and said, "What's wrong? Something bothering you?

Or is it Magnus you're thinking about?"

I didn't say anything.

"You know, some days will be worse than others," Aunt Lillian said. "But it helps to talk about it."

I looked down at my hands. "I don't," I said.

"Don't what?"

"I don't want to talk about it."

"Well, if you change your mind you can always talk to me," she said. "And not just about Magnus. About anything."

"Okay," I said.

She tapped my arm gently. "Now, let me finish cooking your eggs."

The eggs tasted better than anything I had had in a long time. I don't know what was different, but they had these small green bits in them and maybe that was why they tasted so good.

After I had eaten, Aunt Lillian made a salami and cheese sandwich for me to take for lunch. I packed my backpack and put my coat on. Then I put my hood up and walked to school.

My first class was maths. Maths is okay, but the tasks we are given are way too simple and therefore it's also kind of boring.

My maths teacher's name is Steinar Tjelta. He has greyish hair, and he's got small round glasses and he always wears sweater vests. He is really, really old. Definitely over forty. He speaks slow too and that day he was talking about dividing fractions and simplifying fractional expressions. That is really easy and I wished that we could just start solving the maths problems instead of listening to him talk about it. I looked at the clock above the door. It showed the time was 8.32, but it was incorrect. All the clocks in my school show different times.

I looked over at Frida. She was busy taking notes and so were most of the other kids. They didn't seem bored at all. I knew that the clock in my classroom was about three minutes slow, but I wanted to know exactly what time it was, so I decided to check on my phone. I sneaked it out of my jeans pocket and held it under my desk while keeping my eye on Steinar. When he turned to the whiteboard I looked down at my phone. The time was 8.40. I looked up at the clock on the wall, which now showed 8.43. It was two minutes and maybe fifty-seven or fifty-eight seconds slow. There are no digital clocks in my school and it is harder to calculate exact time on a ticking clock. I looked down at my phone and turned the lock screen on and was about to put it back in my pocket when I noticed someone standing next to my desk. It was Steinar. He held out his hand and said, "Give it to me."

"Give you what?"

Steinar sighed. "Give me your phone."

I put my phone in his hand.

"You can have it back after class." Then he put my phone in his desk drawer and went back to talking about dividing fractions and simplifying fractional expressions. It was still one hour, fourteen minutes and twenty-six or twenty-seven seconds until class finished.

We finally started solving some maths problems and it felt good to have something to do. Once you finish the tasks you are given, you are supposed to check that you have got the correct answers before moving on. But I didn't bother checking because I knew that they were right. When it was nine minutes and twenty-one or twenty-two seconds left of class, I had finished all the tasks that Steinar had written on the whiteboard. So I moved on to the next chapter in the book, which was about square roots and prime numbers in calculations. I did six of the problems before I noticed that Steinar was standing next to my desk again.

"What are you doing?" he asked.

"Maths," I said.

Then he put a chubby finger on my maths book and said, "Why are you solving these? This is not what I asked you to do."

Everyone in the classroom turned and looked at us.

Steinar wet his finger with his tongue and flipped back to the previous page. He put his finger in my book again. "These are the ones you are supposed to do. We haven't got to prime numbers in calculations yet."

Then the bell rang and I said, "I need my phone back now."

After class I saw Frida coming out of the toilets down the hall. She walked down the corridor and was probably on her way to meet her friends. I stopped her.

She looked confused. "Oh, hey," she said.

"Did you take my watch?"

She laughed. "What?"

"Did you take my watch?"

Her smile disappeared. "Malin, of course not."

"Did you see who did?"

"No. I mean, where did you have it last?"

"Before swimming class yesterday. After swimming class it was gone."

"Oh no. That's awful. Well, maybe someone has found it. You should check the lost and found. I'll go with you if you want."

Frida walked with me over to the custodian's office. He is the guy who changes the light bulbs and he always has a lot of keys on his belt. No one knows his real name so we just call him the custodian. Frida knocked on the door and the custodian came out. Frida told him that I had lost something and wanted to check the lost and found box.

"Ah, yes," he said and went into the back room. His keys rattled when he walked and I was thinking that a custodian would never be able to sneak up on someone.

When he came back he was carrying a box, which he held out to me.

The box contained some swimming goggles, a flashlight, a yellow flip-flop, some keys and two swimming caps. But no blue and white OTS watch with an analogue and digital display.

"It's not here," I said.

Frida shrugged. "You could always just buy a new one."

But I didn't want a new one. A new watch wouldn't have Magnus's record in it.

Frida smiled. "Hard life, huh?"

"But your life is perfect," I said.

She tilted her head. "What makes you think my life is perfect?"

"You're pretty, and you have a lot of friends and a great family and all the teachers love you."

"There is a lot of pressure with having to be perfect all the time. Everyone expects me to do well on my handball team, and get good marks in school and become prom queen. Honestly, I think you have it a lot easier."

"Why?"

She shrugged. "No one expects anything of you."

## 29

# Family Dinner

When I came home from school that day my house smelled like soap. And in the kitchen all the dirty pans and dishes were gone and everything looked really clean. I sat down at the kitchen table and got started on my homework. At 3.52 p.m. Aunt Lillian came in carrying two full grocery bags. She started putting the food away and asked me, "Do you want pork chops or meatballs for dinner?"

I wasn't really hungry so I said, "I don't know."

Aunt Lillian shrugged. "I might as well make both. They both taste good with gravy and mashed potatoes. Oh, and I am baking an apple cake for dessert."

Maybe it wasn't just old widows who would die to have someone to cook for. Maybe it was women in general.

"A letter came for you today," Aunt Lillian said.

I looked up. "For me?" I couldn't remember the last time I got a letter.

"Yes, it is on the table in the hallway."

I figured the letter would be from my mom, because I don't know anyone who lives far away and she did mention that we could write to each other. But when I saw the envelope I knew straight away that I was wrong. The envelope had a window where my name and address were printed. It was a letter from the medical centre telling me I had an appointment with the physiotherapist.

When I came back into the kitchen Oscar was rubbing his body against Aunt Lillian's legs and purring. He knows very well when someone is dealing with food. Aunt Lillian trimmed some fat off one of the pork chops and put it in his bowl.

"He is not supposed to eat fat," I said.

"Oh, a little fat never harmed anyone," Aunt Lillian said.

At 4.47 Sigve came home. But he wasn't alone. He was with a girl. They came into the kitchen and when Sigve saw our aunt, he said, "Oh."

"Oh, hello," Aunt Lillian said. She wiped her hands on a paper towel and reached her hand out to the girl. "I'm Lillian, Sigve's aunt."

"I am Katrine," the girl said and they shook hands.

"Are you guys hungry? Dinner will be ready soon."

Sigve looked from the girl to Aunt Lillian. "We were actually just gonna make some mac and cheese and head back out again."

"Well, there is plenty of food. I've got pork chops with gravy and mashed potatoes. And meatballs."

They all looked at each other for three seconds and then the girl named Katrine smiled and said, "That sounds great."

I helped Aunt Lillian set the table. She said that we should eat at the dining table in the living room. We normally only eat there at Christmas. Or when we have guests that we don't really know that well. Which I guess we had that day. At 5.16 p.m. Aunt Lillian announced that dinner was ready and we all sat down at the table. Katrine had blonde hair and steel-blue eyes. She looked like someone who had a lot of friends. And who got picked early for teams in PE.

Aunt Lillian put a pork chop on her plate before passing the tray to Katrine. "I've started cleaning out the attic at home," she said. "It is amazing how much crap has piled up over the years." Soon all the trays and bowls were being passed between the four of us. Pork chops, meatballs, mashed potatoes, boiled carrots and lastly the gravy boat.

I was the last person to receive everything, so I had to find room for it all on the table. And I was a bit nervous that I would drop something or spill something. Aunt Lillian said, "I've been thinking about doing a clean-up for years, but I never got around to it. It seemed like the perfect thing to do now that I have some extra time on my hands."

Aunt Lillian had taken some time off from work since Magnus died. That is what she meant by "extra time on her hands". We all started eating while Aunt Lillian continued to talk about cleaning the attic and how she was going to turn it into a study.

The meatballs didn't taste like my mom's. That was a bit strange, because I know they both use Grandma's recipe. They didn't taste bad, but they were different.

At 5.29 p.m. my dad came home. He looked at Katrine and said, "Hello."

"Hello," Katrine said.

"Well, sit down," Aunt Lillian said. "There is plenty of food."

My dad sat down next to me and helped himself to all the food. Then no one really said anything for a while. Everyone was busy cutting and chewing.

"The mash is really good," Katrine said.

"Yes," Aunt Lillian said, "I made it from local potatoes. I bought them at the farmers' market off the main road.

They were very expensive though."

"Potatoes will be on sale at Coop next week," Katrine said.

This made my dad look up from his plate. "You work at the Coop too?"

"Oh, only part-time," Katrine said. "I'm still in school."

"Smart girl." My dad smiled. He pointed his knife at Sigve. "Maybe you could knock some sense into this one. Make him understand the importance of an education."

"Actually," Katrine said, "I think he should do whatever he wants to do."

My dad's smile disappeared. "Oh, is that so?"

Katrine shrugged. "As long as they are not hurting anyone, I think people should do what makes them happy."

My dad scoffed. "A bit of a simple mindset, don't you think?"

"Oh, knock it off," Sigve said. "You are so arrogant."

"Arrogant? How am I arrogant?"

"Just because someone doesn't agree with your way of living, you act like they are worth less than you or something. Everyone has the right to be treated with respect, regardless of their education or income."

Katrine looked down at her plate and started to cut a carrot into smaller pieces.

Then Aunt Lillian said, "Oh God! I completely forgot

about the apple cake." She got up from her chair and hurried into the kitchen.

Katrine continued to cut her carrot into even smaller pieces and my dad started to laugh a low hollow laugh, whilst using his fork to push a piece of pork chop around in the pool of gravy on his plate.

"What the hell are you laughing about?" Sigve said.

"Nothing. I just didn't know my son was a hippy, is all."

Sigve scoffed. "What does that even mean?"

I said, "A hippy is someone who protested against the materialistic society in the 1960s. They were against the military and any use of weapons and they took a lot of drugs and wore colourful clothes. Their motto was, 'Make love, not war.'"

Everyone turned and looked at me. After four seconds my dad said, "You will have to excuse me, I have some work to do." He pushed his chair back from the table and left the room.

Katrine, who had finally finished dissecting her carrot, now used her fork to push the pieces backwards and forwards on the plate.

I said, "Are you Sigve's girlfriend?"

Katrine looked up from her plate and laughed a sudden loud laugh that ended as quickly as it started. She looked at Sigve. "Wow, time sure flies when you're having fun," she said. She put her hand on Sigve's shoulder. "I should get going." She got up from her chair, and gently stroked Sigve's arm before leaving.

We heard the front door opening and closing.

"Is she your girlfriend?" I said.

Sigve didn't answer. Instead he said, "Why do you always have to be so fucking weird?" Then he got up and left too.

Aunt Lillian came in with the apple cake and said, "Where is everyone?"

"Gone," I said.

She put the cake on the table.

"Ah, well, more for us," she said.

"I don't like apple cake," I said.

"Oh, well, more for me then," she said and sat down in her chair. I was wondering if she was going to cut herself a piece of the cake, because the only plate she had still had pork chops and gravy on it.

"Well, I should probably head home soon," she said. "I had this guy install a new lamp in the attic today, I can't wait to see what it looks like."

"He's been at your house while you've been here? All alone?"

"Oh, yeah, I kind of know him from way back. I trust him."

"But how do you know who to trust?"

"Oh, I trust everyone until they give me a reason not to."

# 30

# Physical Therapy

The physiotherapy place smelled like mouthwash. I had to walk up three flights of stairs to get there and I could smell it even before I entered the room. I pushed open the heavy glass door and walked up to the counter, where a lady was sitting. She had red curly hair and glasses hanging from a string around her neck. I told her that I had an appointment.

She put her glasses on and said, "What is your name?"

"Malin Sande."

"All right. And why are you here today?"

"I received a letter."

"No, I mean what is the problem?"

"My shoulder."

She typed something into her computer and then she

asked me to have a seat and I did. There was no one else in the waiting room but me. There were four chairs, a coat stand and a health magazine from six years ago. The walls were white and there were no pictures.

Two minutes and eleven seconds later a man in sports leggings showed up. He shook my hand and told me his name was Audun. His hand was cold and smooth. He nodded, signalling for me to follow him, and we walked into the training room.

The room had a couple of exercise bikes and some other machines that I didn't really know the use of. There were also weights and some of those big exercise balls.

The only two people in there were an old lady, who was lying on a mat on the floor, and a physiotherapist (at least I guessed he was a physiotherapist), who was helping her bend her knee.

Audun led the way to some chairs and told me I could sit down if I wanted and I did.

"So why did you ask for a physiotherapy session?" he said.

"I didn't. The doctor did."

He looked at me for a couple of seconds. "Okay… And what is the problem?"

"I dislocated my shoulder. Twice."

"How did you do that?"

"The first time I fell off my bike. And the second time I tried to hit a volleyball over the net. I wasn't successful."

"I see," he said.

Then he asked me more questions about how old I was and how much time had passed since my injuries and what treatment I had been given.

"All right," he said. "We will be doing some exercises today. You need to build up the muscles around your shoulder so that it stays in place." He started walking and signalled for me to follow him. He led me over to the exercise bikes.

"First we need to warm up," he said. He told me that I should bike for ten to fifteen minutes to get warm.

I got on the bike and Audun started pushing buttons on the display and set the timer for fifteen minutes.

"I will be back," he said, and then he left.

I started pedalling and found it really boring straight away. Why would anyone get on a bike that didn't take them anywhere?

Audun came back after twelve minutes and fifty-nine seconds.

"How are you doing?" he said.

"Fine," I said.

"Are you feeling warm yet?"

"Yes."

"Good, you can stop now if you want."

I got off the bike and Audun held up a piece of paper. "I have made an exercise programme for you. You need to do these every day in order to get better. We will get started now and I will show you how to do them." I didn't know why he kept saying "we" when I was the only one doing any work.

The programme consisted of me lifting dumb-bells that were only a kilo each. And there were several ways I could lift these to help build muscles. If I didn't have dumb-bells at home I could use milk cartons. Or water bottles. Then he showed me some exercises where I pulled a resistance band in different directions. He advised me to buy one of these bands.

"Do you do any sports?" he said.

"No."

"Hmm."

Lastly he showed me some exercises on the mat. Push-ups and other ways for me to stretch and put a little pressure on my shoulder.

After our session he gave me the sheet with the exercises on. They were all explained in detail with pictures.

"Now, I want you to pick three of these exercises every day and do each three times, ten seconds each time. Every day."

"Okay," I said and accepted the sheet.

"Good," he said. "The receptionist has gone home for the day, so call in tomorrow morning to make a new appointment."

"Okay," I said.

When I got home my house didn't smell like dinner. Or soap. So I figured Aunt Lillian wasn't there. The house was quiet so I guessed no one else was home either. I turned the TV on and lay down on the floor to do some of the exercises I had been given. I did two push-ups, but they were too exhausting and I was tired. I went into the kitchen and got a milk carton and started lifting it the way the physiotherapist had showed me. I looked at the clock above the door as I was doing it so that I could keep track of the time. I lifted it for ten seconds, waited, and started from the beginning. It was pretty boring and my mind drifted off. I wondered when my mom was going to call that day.

Then Sigve stood in the doorway. I hadn't heard him come in.

"What the hell are you doing?" he said.

"Not much," I said and put the milk carton on the counter. "I am wondering when Mom will call. From her business trip."

"Business trip?" Sigve sneered. "You don't actually believe that she is on a business trip, do you?"

"What do you mean?"

Sigve picked up an apple from the counter. "Oh, nothing." He nodded at the fridge. "Hey, get the juice carton out next, will you? It could use some airing too." Then he bit into the apple and left the room. Shortly after I could hear him running down the stairs to the basement.

I put the milk carton back in the fridge and went into the living room and turned on the TV. They were showing an old episode of *Prison Break*.

At 5.37 p.m. my dad came home carrying a grocery bag. I don't think I have ever seen my dad with a grocery bag before.

"Hello," he said.

"Hello," I said. "What time will Mom be calling today?"

"She won't."

"Why not?"

"She is having a hard time at the moment. She needs some time to herself."

"Why?"

My dad sighed and stroked his moustache a couple of times. "It is too hard for her to talk to us when she is not able to see us or come home. She just needs some time. It will all be fine."

He reached into the grocery bag and took out a microwave dinner box.

"Chicken curry?" he said.

I nodded and he disappeared into the kitchen.

My mom was having a hard time and she wasn't able to come home. I thought about what Sigve had said. He'd made it sound like my mom wasn't on a business trip. But if that was true, then where was she?

I looked at the screen and watched the bald guy talk to some other guy about their plan to escape.

Maybe my mom was in prison?

At 5.47 Sigve came up from the basement and sat down on the couch. I handed him the remote but he waved it away. "It's fine," he said.

Then my dad said that dinner was ready and we all decided that it would be a good idea to eat in front of the TV.

We watched some of the guys in *Prison Break* argue about something, but I couldn't really catch what they were talking about. It is hard to follow if you don't see every episode.

"Is Mom in prison?" I said.

Sigve started choking on a piece of chicken and my dad knocked his glass of water over.

"What the hell are you saying?" my dad said.

"Is Mom in prison?" I repeated. "I mean, it would explain why I can't call her and why she is not allowed to come home yet."

My dad exhaled deeply. "No, Mom is not in prison." He started wiping up the water with some paper towels. "She will be home soon. On the twentieth of April. You know this already. Everything will be fine. Now eat your food."

The twentieth of April was thirty-seven days, five hours and forty-six minutes away. I wasn't sure what to believe, because no one tells me anything anyway. If I knew the address of where she was staying I could have sent her the cigarettes that Hanna left that time.

Maybe they could be used as currency. Wherever she was.

## 31

# Clockwork

I worked out the actual time of all the clocks in my school. I compared them with the clock on my mobile phone to see how much faster or slower they were. Then I noted it all down in the back of my notebook.

This is what I wrote:

*My classroom: three minutes and fifty-eight seconds slow*

*Science lab: six minutes and forty-two seconds fast*

*Arts and crafts room: one minute and eleven seconds slow*

*Gym: four minutes and fifty-four seconds slow*

*Library: two minutes and fifty-nine seconds slow*

Now, instead of checking my mobile every time I wanted to know what time it was, I could just look at the clock and check the actual time in my notebook. I checked all the clocks during my lunch break so I wouldn't risk having my mobile taken away from me again.

Afterwards, I sat down on the floor outside my classroom and took out my encyclopedia and opened it to a random page. It said:

### Slang:

Deliberate deviations from ordinary language. Very informal and often more metaphorical and playful than regular language. What is considered slang changes over time.

Then I got distracted because I heard someone laughing. It was a laugh that I recognized, but hadn't heard in a while. I looked up and saw Ruben. He was talking to that girl again. The one with the blonde curly hair.

Then someone said, "Hello."

And I turned around and looked up at Frida. "Hello," I said.

"What are you doing?"

"Reading."

She smiled. "Bit hard to read without looking at your book, isn't it?"

Frida took my coat, which was lying next to me, and

folded it neatly on the floor before she sat down on it.

"Is it okay if I sit on your coat?" she said.

"Okay."

"So, are you going to the prom?"

"I don't know," I said.

"But you have to go. It will be fun."

At the prom you need to wear a fancy dress. And there is dancing. I don't think I would like it.

I said, "I don't think so."

"This will be your best chance of fixing things with Ruben." She nodded in his direction. "Boys like girls when they are all dressed up."

"But I don't have anything to wear."

"Well, you need to buy a new dress, of course. Everyone buys a new dress for the prom. I have a blue evening gown on hold at Stitch and a silver one at Stusio. I haven't decided which one I will get yet."

I didn't know either of those places. I wasn't even sure that I knew what an evening gown was.

"Oh, and I really wanted to make up for accidentally saying what I said to Ruben. To show you how sorry I am, you are invited to my house before the prom," Frida said. "Me and Norunn and Julie are all meeting at my place to get ready. And my dad will drive us there."

I looked down at my book.

## Snake:

Any reptile of the suborder Serpentes, characterized by elongated limbless bodies. Can also refer to a non-trustworthy person, i.e. an enemy.

"So you are coming, right?" Frida said.

"Okay," I whispered.

"Good." She pointed at my book. "What is that anyway?"

I closed it and showed her the cover.

She looked at it and said, "I don't remember that being part of the curriculum."

"It's not."

Then the bell rang.

When I got home my house smelled like food. And not a frozen pizza or microwaved ready meal, but real food. That meant that Aunt Lillian was there.

My dad came home at 5.43 p.m. and the three of us sat down to eat. Sigve wasn't there, because he was having dinner at a friend's house. I wondered if the friend was Katrine. We had pancakes with bacon and potatoes, which I really love.

Oscar was meowing and begging for food under the table. I slipped him small pieces of bacon when no one was looking. A little fat never harmed anyone.

"How is the food?" Aunt Lillian said.

"Good," I said.

Aunt Lillian looked at my dad. "What do you think, Leif," she said. "Is the food all right?"

"It is okay," he said.

"Just okay?"

He shrugged. "Sometimes okay is enough."

And then none of us said much more.

After dinner I went into my room and opened the encyclopedia on a random page. It said:

### Dress:

Clothing for women with skirt and bodice in one piece. A dress can be formal or informal.

That reminded me. I needed a dress.

I went into the living room where my dad was watching TV.

"I need a dress," I said.

"What? Why?"

"For prom."

"What prom?"

"At my school. We are having a prom and I need a dress."

"Oh." He stroked his moustache. "But don't you already have a dress? What about the one that you wore to the funeral?"

"But Frida says that everyone buys a new dress for the prom."

Then Aunt Lillian came in, wiping her hands on a kitchen towel. "Leif, don't be silly, of course she needs a new dress. It is her first prom."

My dad grunted and turned up the volume on the TV.

Aunt Lillian looked at me and smiled. "I will help you pick it out."

# 32

## The Prom Crew

Frida told me that she and the rest of the prom committee were having one more meeting before the event to get all the last-minute details sorted. And as I was now part of their "prom crew", as she called it, I was invited too. It was very important that I came so that I got all the information.

I had been kind of lonely lately and I figured it would be nice to hang out with someone for a change. So I accepted the invitation. My guard was up though. If they asked me to steal anything, I wasn't going to do it.

The committee consisted of Frida, Julie and Norunn and the meeting was held at Frida's house after school.

We were all sitting in the upstairs living room. The couch in this room was grey and there were tons of cushions on it. Some had pictures of animals like owls and reindeers. And some had quotes on them, like *Live, Laugh, Love*. One of the walls was covered with bookshelves, and there were candlesticks everywhere. On another wall there was a huge TV.

But we weren't there to watch TV. We were there to talk about the prom. The prom was twelve days, three hours and fifty-six minutes away. I had no idea why we needed to talk about it now.

"Okay," Frida said, "I have decided on a dress. I'm gonna go for the blue one."

"Oh, I was hoping you'd go for that one," Julie said.

"Yes," Norunn agreed. "You looked absolutely stunning in that dress. I mean, you looked stunning in both of them, but, yeah, you know what I mean."

"Right," Frida said. "So no one can wear a blue dress to the prom, okay? It would look really stupid if we all wore the same colour." Frida locked eyes with me just a bit longer than seemed necessary.

Then she turned her attention to her phone, which had started beeping. And Julie and Norunn looked at their phones as well.

"I can't wait," Frida said. "It will be the most memorable night of our lives."

The others agreed.

"What are you gonna do with your hair, Frida?" Norunn asked.

"Well, the original plan was to put it up in a bun on top of my head. But," she said and took a long pause, "as my hair is much shorter now, I think I will curl it instead. I've watched different YouTube videos that show how to do it."

Julie turned and looked at me.

"What are you gonna do with your hair, Malin?"

Then there was a knock on the door and Frida's mom came in. She held out a tray and said: "I've brought some cheese and crackers for you girls."

Frida rolled her eyes and sighed. "Mom, we don't want crackers. Bring us some carrots and dip or something."

"But you love these."

"No, I don't. That was, like, two months ago."

"Oh," her mom said and slowly backed out with the tray.

Then Frida turned to me and said, "So, I haven't seen you with that girl in ages. What's her name again?"

"Hanna," I said.

"That's it. Are you not friends any more?"

"I don't think so. Last time I saw her, she showed me her middle finger."

This made them all laugh.

"That doesn't surprise me," Frida said. "She doesn't seem like a very nice person. And she smokes too."

"That's not true," I said. "She quit when she got pregnant."

They laughed again.

Frida looked at me. "You don't smoke, do you?"

"No," I said. "Do you?"

"God, no! They stain your teeth. And they are really bad for your skin."

Frida's mom came back in and this time she brought carrots and broccoli and a little bowl with some white stuff that looked like sour cream. "Enjoy," she said and walked out. The girls helped themselves to the vegetables and dipped them in the white stuff. They were quiet for a while as they dipped and chewed. Frida pushed the bowls closer to me so I could reach them. I helped myself to a carrot and dipped it like the others did. The dip tasted like nothing with an aftertaste of lemon zest.

"This is really good," Julie said. The other two agreed.

"So, did you find your watch?" Frida asked me.

"No."

"It was weird how it just disappeared like that."

"Are you sure you brought it to school that day?" Norunn said. "I mean, maybe you left it at home or something."

"I did bring it to school. I had it just before swimming class. After class it was gone."

"Super weird," Julie said.

I finished my carrot. I didn't understand why someone would put dip on a carrot, because it made it taste worse. To be honest, I didn't really see the point of sitting around eating carrots anyway. As soon as I finished, Frida held out the bowl to me again and I helped myself to another one. I was about to put it in my mouth when Frida said, "Wait, you need to put dip on it." I gently dipped it in the white stuff and tried to get as little as possible on it.

"When are you going to buy a dress for the prom?" Frida asked me.

"I don't know."

"Well, you'd better hurry. All the good ones get taken early."

"Oh God," Julie said. "Do you remember that dress Emilie wore to my birthday party last year?"

This made Frida and Norunn laugh. "That was hideous," Norunn said.

"I heard she bought it second-hand," Frida said.

Then they all got busy with their phones again. I was starting to feel a little nauseous from the dip. I wondered how I could get rid of the carrot without anyone noticing. And then, out of the blue, Norunn turned to me and said,

224

"So what is going on between you and Ruben anyway?"

"What?" I said.

"Are you dating or something?" Julie said.

"No," I said.

"Were you?" Frida said.

"We were friends."

"But you wanted to be more than friends, right?"

I didn't say anything. It didn't matter how I felt about Ruben, because he was upset with me. He thought I found him weird and gross.

"Don't worry," Frida said. "He will change his mind when he sees you in your dress. If you get the right one, of course."

She held out one of the bowls to me. "Broccoli?"

# 33

# Dress

Aunt Lillian said that dress shopping would be fun. This was a lie. Grown-ups tell a lot of lies when it comes to things like this. But I did need help picking out a dress, because I had no idea how to find "the right one".

Aunt Lillian picked me up at my house at 11.02 a.m. on a Saturday to take me to the shopping centre in Bryne. M44 has more than sixty stores where you can purchase all of your daily needs. That is what their website says anyway.

On our way over, Aunt Lillian was really chatty as usual.

"So, you must be excited about going to your first prom?"

I wasn't. A part of me hoped that I would get sick so I wouldn't have to go. But there was also a part of me that hoped I would get to talk to Ruben. Maybe Frida was right.

Maybe he would like me again if he saw me in a dress. Frida knows a lot about boys.

"We didn't have proms when I grew up," Aunt Lillian said, "but we did have dances in the old barn in Nesvik. Every other Friday night. It was really exciting, getting dressed up, listening to music, maybe dancing with a boy you liked."

"Is that how you met Magnus's dad?" I said.

And that was when Aunt Lillian almost hit a pigeon and we stopped talking about the dance.

We pulled up in the parking lot at M44 at 11.21 a.m. and took the escalator up to the first floor, where all the clothing stores are. Aunt Lillian said that we should work our way through all the stores from left to right.

When we walked into the first store a lady greeted us and said, "How may I help you today?"

Aunt Lillian looked at me and said, "We are looking for a dress. For a first prom."

"Oh, well, we have plenty of evening gowns that can be used for lots of different occasions," the lady said. She led us over to a section which had several dresses and started talking about the differences between them. I wasn't really listening though, because a dress on the rack closest to me had caught my eye.

It was in a tan colour, which isn't really my favourite,

but it had a nice pattern at the very bottom. It looked like tree branches in different shapes and sizes that were wrapped around the dress. It was beautiful.

"Want to try it on?" Aunt Lillian said.

"Yes," I said.

Above the rack was a poster that showed the price of the dress, and it had a picture of a girl wearing it. She had one hand on her waist and in the other she was holding a clutch bag. Her mouth was slightly open, like she was inhaling. Or exhaling. She couldn't be much older than me, but the dress made her look mature and sophisticated. Then I put it on and I looked like a sack of potatoes.

I stood in the changing room and looked at myself in the mirror. The exact same dress that looked so perfect a couple of minutes ago now looked completely different. Maybe this was why it was called a changing room. Maybe the clothes changed in there.

Then I heard the lady's voice. "How's it going in there?" And when I didn't answer, she tugged the curtains a couple of times and said, "Are you okay?"

Why wouldn't I be okay? What could go wrong in a changing room?

Then I heard Aunt Lillian's voice. "Can we see?"

I pulled the curtains to one side.

"Oh, that is lovely," the lady said.

"Maybe we should try on a few more," Aunt Lillian said.

I tried on several dresses that I thought were either nice, very nice or just okay on their hangers. Green, gold, purple, ruffles, straight, short, long. All kinds. And when I put them on, they all looked terrible. Or maybe it was me. Maybe I looked terrible. In any case, when I looked in the mirror all I could see was me wearing something that didn't fit me right. They looked unfamiliar and alien. And wrong.

"What about this one?"

I looked at the dress Aunt Lillian was holding. It was a long strapless dress in deep red. And it had a wide belt at the waist. It was awful. I decided to try it on anyway. Maybe the dresses that looked ugly in the store would look better once I put them on. It didn't.

It felt like we had been through all the dresses in the store. Then Aunt Lillian held up a blue dress. The bottom half was wider and in a darker blue than the top half. Even though it was a dress. It looked more like a top and a skirt that were attached to each other. It was pretty. But I couldn't have a blue dress. Frida had said so.

"Not blue," I said.

Aunt Lillian looked at the dress and then looked at me. "But you love blue?"

"That was two months ago," I said.

I was tired of trying on dresses and I wanted to go home and watch TV and have a snack. "Maybe we should go home," I said.

Aunt Lillian laughed. "Oh, it is way too early to throw in the towel already. There are plenty of other stores to go to."

We went into three more shops, but they didn't have a lot of dresses and I didn't try anything on. In the end I found a dress in two different grey tones that looked okay. And when I tried it on it still looked okay. So we decided to buy it. Sometimes okay is enough.

I was happy that I'd found a dress, but I was even happier that the shopping was over. Now I could go home and relax for the rest of the day. If we left straight away I could catch *One Tree Hill* reruns on TV.

"Now we need to find shoes," Aunt Lillian said.

# 34

# Preparations

On the day of the prom I went over to Frida's house like we had agreed. The prom started at 7 p.m. and Frida said to be at her house at 4 p.m., because then we could take our time getting ready, and have snacks and chat and have fun.

Frida said not to put the dress on until I got to her house or else it would get wrinkled in the car. That didn't really make sense though, because Frida's dad was going to drive us to the prom, which would mean the dress would get wrinkled anyway. But I did what she said. It is just easier sometimes.

I put my dress and my tights in a plastic bag and Aunt Lillian drove me over to Frida's house. At 3.58 p.m. I rang the doorbell and Frida's mom opened the door. She showed me to the downstairs living room, where Frida, Julie and Norunn were sitting on the very white couch. They were all there already even though the time was only 3.59 p.m. On the table was a bowl of strawberries, a bottle of something that looked like champagne and four long-stemmed glasses.

"Help yourself to cider and strawberries," Frida's mom said.

"No! Not yet, Mom," Frida shouted. "God, I haven't even taken a photo of it yet."

"Oh dear, I'm sorry."

"You can leave now," Frida said.

Frida's mom smiled and left the room.

"How are you, Malin?" Frida said.

"I'm okay," I said.

Frida went and picked up one of those big SLR cameras and started taking pictures of the table. She probably took over ten pictures and she didn't change the angle or anything. She just kept clicking the button and taking identical pictures over and over again.

Then she opened the cider and poured it into the glasses. The label said *Herrljunga Magnum Cider. Alcohol free*. Then she put a strawberry in each of the glasses. I reached my hand out to pick one of them up, but Frida stopped me by shouting, "Not yet!" She got the camera out again and started taking a bunch of pictures of this as well.

Frida handed me the camera. "Can you take a picture of us?" The girls each picked up a glass, put one hand on their hips and puckered their lips. I took the picture and lowered the camera.

"You need to take more," Frida said.

I held up the camera again and pushed the button over and over.

"Now I can take a picture of you," Frida said. She handed me the fourth glass and took the camera from me. And then she took five or maybe six pictures of me. Then we all sat down on the white couch and we were allowed to drink our cider. It was lukewarm and tasted no different from apple juice.

At 4.16 p.m. Frida said that it was getting late and we needed to hurry up and get ready, so we went into her room to get changed. It was two hours, forty-three minutes and nineteen seconds until the prom started.

Frida's room was huge. Along one wall there was a white dressing table and above it a big mirror with a golden frame. Around the edge of the mirror there were some photos of herself and her friends. Next to the dressing table was a clothing rack that looked like the ones you would see in a shop and there were different blouses hanging on it. She also had a big closet and a desk and a small couch. On her bed lay three garment bags.

The girls got their dresses out of the bags. Norunn's dress was in a deep red colour and the top half sparkled with silver.

"Oh, I can't wait to see you in your dress," Frida said. "Red really suits you."

"Yes, and I got the shoes too." Norunn picked up a pair of shoes by the bed. They were also red with some silver details.

Frida and Julie both squealed and were really excited about that.

Julie's dress was gold and she also had matching golden shoes and a golden clutch bag. And Norunn and Frida talked about how pretty that one was as well. And how much it would suit her.

Frida let her hands run down her blue dress.

"It is stunning," Julie said.

"Perfect," Norunn said.

"I am really excited to wear a Faviana dress for the first time," Frida said.

Julie turned to me. "Who are you wearing, Malin?"

I didn't know what she meant so I didn't answer. I took my grey dress out of my bag and held it up for them to see.

"Oh, that one looks super gorgeous," Frida said.

"It really does," the others agreed.

"And it is grey so it will make you blend in more," Julie said. "Then people won't notice those wide straps, which aren't really in style at the moment."

"Perfect," Norunn said.

We all changed into our dresses. I took my jumper and T-shirt off and pulled the dress on over my head. Then I took my shoes and socks and jeans off and put on my tights before putting my shoes back on. And there I was, all ready. And it was still two hours and eleven minutes until the prom started.

I sat down on the couch and wondered what we were going to do next. Frida sat down in front of the dressing table and picked up a small box and a brush. She opened the lid and dipped the brush and proceeded to apply it to her eyelids, making them blue. "Too much?" she asked.

"No, just enough," Julie said.

"Perfect," Norunn said.

The other girls squashed together in front of the mirror and went through the same procedure, turning their eyelids the same colour as their dresses. After that, they all used these pens to draw lines around their eyes, talking about how they all needed just the right shade to suit their individual needs, even though they all looked the same colour to me. They finished off by applying mascara to their lashes and they had a lot of thoughts on this subject too. One of them had a mascara that created an illusion of length and one had a mascara that added volume. Or something. I was very bored.

Just when I thought they were done, they needed to do their hair too. Norunn used a curling iron and turned Frida's perfect hair into perfect curls while Frida made sure she did it correctly by following a YouTube video on an iPad. After that, Julie and Norunn both put their hair up in tight buns on top of their heads, which made them look like stewardesses.

When they were all done with their hair, Frida texted her mom and asked her to bring us more cider. And then I had to take another picture of them holding their champagne glasses while they were all dressed up.

Afterwards, we went into the living room and Frida's mom took a photo of Frida standing by the front door. Then she took pictures of Frida and Julie, then Frida and Julie and Norunn, and finally she took some pictures of all four of us.

Frida said, "Just wait until you see the gym, it is so pretty with all the decorations and everything. You are not even going to recognize it."

Then we all got in the car and headed off for the most memorable night of our lives.

# 35

# Prom

At 6.47 p.m. we walked into the gym of Haasund Lower Secondary School. There were streamers hanging from the wall bars and from the basketball baskets. The entire room had been decorated with blue and silver balloons. By one of the walls was a long table, with a blue tablecloth with silver stars printed on it. On the table there were several bowls of punch and different types of snacks. On each side of the room there were several smaller tables for people to sit at. They all had the same blue tablecloths. In the middle of the room was a huge empty space, which Frida said was the dance floor.

It still looked like the gym though. Only now it had balloons and streamers.

Over by the stage I saw Trude Fjell and Principal Skogen and some of the moms who are always here for these kinds of things. They were the chaperones for the evening.

Apart from them, we were the only ones who had arrived.

Frida said we needed to hang our coats in the locker rooms, but my phone was in the pocket of my coat and I didn't want to leave it.

Frida looked at me and said in a strict voice, "You have to hang your coat."

I didn't answer.

"No one wears a coat inside the ballroom. Stop ruining the prom."

So I went down to the locker room with the girls and hung up my coat. I took my phone out of the pocket and carried it in my hand.

When we came back upstairs, more and more people were arriving. As they walked in, the boys went and sat at tables on the right side of the room, while the girls went to the left side. I didn't see anyone from the tenth grade. Only kids from my year and the year below us.

One of the tables was still free and Frida led the way over to that one.

When we got closer I saw that it had a sign. It said, *Reserved*.

We sat down and Frida immediately ordered Julie and Norunn to fetch us drinks and snacks. As they left, Frida turned to me. She nodded towards the table next to ours. "Did you see Marta?" I turned and looked at her. She was wearing a strapless dress in dark green. "Look at that colour," Frida said. "Who would wear a dress like that?"

Norunn and Julie came back. They put four plastic champagne glasses of punch on the table, together with a small bowl of peanuts.

They sat down and Julie said, "We met Camilla over by the snack table. Did you see her dress?" We all turned and looked, but I wasn't sure who Camilla was.

"Look at those wide straps," Norunn said. "They are so not in style any more."

They all chuckled.

I crossed my arms over my chest. I wished I had my coat on so I could cover the straps of my dress.

Then the girl who apparently was Camilla made her way over to our table.

"Hello," she said.

Frida got up from her seat and gave her a hug.

"I'm glad you could make it," Frida said. "Oh, and I love your dress."

"It's beautiful," Norunn said.

"Yes." Julie nodded. "It really is."

"Thanks, you all look great too," Camilla said. "Well, I'd better get back to my table." And she left.

That's when I noticed Ruben. He was talking to some of his friends over by the snack table. He had a blue suit on. And a bow tie. His hair was slightly messy. But in a good way. He looked happy.

The music started playing, but no one was dancing. Everyone just sat at the tables or stood in groups, eating snacks and drinking punch. Frida and the girls kept commenting on everyone's outfits.

At 7.51 p.m. I went downstairs to use the toilet. And when I went to wash my hands, Trude walked in.

"Hello, Malin," Trude said.

"Hello."

"You look lovely in that dress."

Trude was wearing a peach skirt suit. According to Frida, only people over sixty wore peach-coloured clothes. I wondered how old Trude was.

"How is your night going?" Trude said.

"Okay," I said.

"Well, enjoy it. You know, your first prom is something that you will remember for ever."

I wiped my hands and walked out.

On the other side of the door I accidentally bumped into a boy.

"Oh, sorry," he said.

It was Ruben.

I smiled. "Hello."

Ruben didn't smile. He said, "Just so you know, I don't like you either!" And then he walked away. He pushed the door to the boys' toilet open and left it swinging backwards and forwards after him.

Frida was wrong. Ruben didn't care if I was wearing a dress.

When I walked back up, Frida was waiting for me at the top of the stairs.

"Did you vote yet?" she said.

"What?"

"Did you vote yet? For prom queen?"

"No."

"Well, now is a good time to do it, isn't it?"

I shrugged. "I guess."

She looked at me. "I think we both know who you will be voting for."

She didn't blink.

"You owe me that much," she said.

The voting took place in the room where we keep all the sports equipment. Someone had set up a few partitions to shield the voting table. Outside stood Principal Skogen and he handed me a pink ballot paper and a blue ballot paper. Inside there was a table and on it was a box with a padlock and a hole to put your vote in. Next to it was a bunch of pens.

I looked at the pink ballot. It had three names – Julie, Frida and Norunn – and next to each of the names there was a box for you to tick. I didn't actually care which one of them won the title, but I supposed that I should vote for Frida, because apparently I owed her that much. But then I thought about Ruben and how Frida explained to me that boys like prom queens and it made me unsure of what I should do. I didn't want Ruben to like any of those girls. So under the names I made a new box, which I ticked. And next to the box I wrote a new name: *Trude Fjell*.

The blue ballot was for the prom king. I didn't realize that we were voting for a king as well. The candidates were:

Gjermund Moen.

Vegard Gudmestad.

And Ruben Oftedal.

I didn't know who to vote for. I didn't want Vegard or Gjermund to win, because they are not nice. But I wanted Ruben to win least of all. If he became king he would probably dance with whoever was made prom queen. And maybe they would fall in love. I decided to leave that ballot blank. I just folded it and put it into the box.

When I walked back out, quite a few people had made it onto the dance floor. There were no couples dancing though. People just danced in groups. Frida, Norunn and Julie were dancing too. I sat back down at the table and ate peanuts and watched the people on the dance floor.

At 8.31 p.m. the music stopped and Trude went up onstage. She grabbed the mic and said that it was time to announce the prom king and queen. Then there was a lot of feedback from the microphone and everyone covered their ears.

Principal Skogen rushed up onstage and fiddled with some buttons. Then Trude started talking again.

"It was a close race, but we have a winner," she said. "The prom queen of Haasund Lower Secondary School's first prom is…" Trude paused and looked out at the crowd, who were now completely silent. Then she said, "Frida Berg."

Frida gasped and looked completely surprised. She was so surprised she even started gasping half a second before her name was announced. Everyone clapped and Frida quickly hugged Norunn and Julie before rushing up onstage.

Trude took the mic again and said, "But as we all know, every queen needs a king. And the king of Haasund Lower Secondary School's first prom is…Ruben Oftedal."

I looked over at Ruben. He smiled a shy smile, while his friends patted his back and punched him lightly on the shoulder. Then he went up onstage and stood next to Frida, and some girls who I didn't know came out from backstage and put crowns on top of their heads and ribbons with their new titles across their chests. Trude held the mic out to Frida. "Would you like to say anything?"

"I would just like to say that this was all really unexpected and I haven't prepared a speech or anything, but I would like to thank you all for voting for me, and you are all so amazing and beautiful and I can't believe you gave the title to me. You are the best." Everyone clapped again, and Trude passed the mic to Ruben.

"Thank you," he said.

The music started playing again and people continued dancing. Frida and Ruben walked out to the dance floor too, but they didn't dance with each other like I have seen prom king and queens do on TV. They just went back to dancing with their friends like before.

I looked over at Ruben. The crown was a bit too big for his head and he had to keep pushing it back.

The bowl of peanuts was nearly empty when Frida came over to the table.

"Hello," she said.

"Hello."

"I just wanted to thank you for voting for me."

I didn't answer.

"Every vote counts in these kinds of situations. Like Trude said, it was a close race. And I know you and me haven't always seen eye to eye in the past, so I just wanted to say thanks."

Suddenly I made eye contact with Ruben. His smile disappeared and he looked the other way.

Frida said, "I could talk to him for you if you want?"

There wasn't much time left. The prom ended at 9.30 p.m. and it was already 9.23. I watched Frida make her way towards Ruben. I looked at the time on my phone and wished she would walk a little bit faster. I saw her tapping his shoulder and she said something that I could not hear, but he was smiling, so that was a good sign. As the prom was ending more and more people were making their way towards the exit and soon they blocked my view, so I couldn't see Frida and Ruben any more. Then Principal Skogen came over to my table and said that it was time for the clean-up committee to clear away the tables.

I looked at him.

"It is time to leave, Malin," he said.

I made my way across the room and went downstairs to get my coat.

When I came back upstairs I looked for Frida and

Ruben, but they were lost in the crowd and I couldn't see them anywhere.

I went outside and after a few seconds I heard someone behind me say, "Malin."

I turned around. It was Frida.

She said, "Are you ready to leave?"

"What did he say?"

"Who?"

"Ruben."

"Oh, that's right. I almost forgot." She started looking for something in her bag. "He asked me to give you this." She held out a note for me.

I opened the note and read it. It said, *Meet me in the toilet behind the gym at 9.45. Ruben.*

"So are you coming?" Frida asked. "My dad is waiting."

"No," I said, "I will go home by myself."

"Okay," Frida said. And then she walked down the stairs and she and the girls drove off in her dad's car.

I sat down on the step and looked at my mobile. It was 9.39 p.m.

At 9.45 sharp I opened the door to the toilets. My heart was beating really fast as I walked in. It was completely dark and it smelled like a mixture of wet metal and a sewer.

"Hello?" I said.

I turned the lights on, but I couldn't see anyone. I was about to check the cubicles, but then I noticed the envelope that was lying in the middle of the floor. It had *Malin* written on it.

I opened it in a hurry and took out the note inside. The note said, *If you want your watch back, come to the large oak tree in Naerheim Woods, tonight, at 10 p.m.*

# 36

# Cut Scene

It felt like I had been kicked in the stomach. Ruben had my watch? Maybe he took it when he was mad at me and now that Frida had talked to him he wanted to give it back? A lot of things were running through my head, but I knew one thing for sure: I was getting my watch back.

I hurried down Torg Street, holding onto my dress to avoid stepping on it. I turned and ran down Valen Street, past Holberg's shop. My shoes were pinching my toes so I had to slow down for a while. It was really dark outside and even though I know Haasund really well and no real crime ever happens it was a bit scary to be out so late by myself. I was half-walking, half-running up Haugen Hill and only two thoughts were going through my mind:

*my watch, Ruben, my watch, Ruben.* And then I thought: *Magnus's record. Would it still be there?*

When I arrived at Naerheim Woods nine minutes and fifty-nine seconds later, I was pretty much exhausted. I tried to calm down and walk slowly so I could catch my breath, but again my heart was beating so fast and I felt really nervous. I approached the oak tree but I couldn't see Ruben anywhere. I had never been to the woods so late at night before. It wasn't completely dark because of the lamp posts, but it was still kind of creepy. I pulled my coat tighter around me and waited for Ruben to appear. Apart from the chaperones and the cleaners, I'd been the last one to leave the prom, so he should have been here by now.

Then I heard a rustling in the bushes over by the pine trees and I turned around. It was not Ruben.

It was Frida, and Julie and Norunn. They were still all dressed up. Frida even had her tiara and ribbon on and she was holding something behind her back that I couldn't see.

"Well, hello," Frida said.

"Where is Ruben?" I said.

"Ruben?" They all looked at each other and laughed.

"Yes, Ruben asked me to meet him here."

"You really thought Ruben would actually come to see you?"

This made them all laugh again.

"God," Frida said, "you are even dumber than I thought." She smiled, but her eyes were dead. Like two lava stones.

Julie reached into her clutch bag and held something up for me to see. "Are you looking for this?"

It was my watch.

"That's mine," I said. "Give it to me."

"Don't worry," Frida said. "You will get it in due time. But first there is something else we need to take care of."

She took her hand out from behind her back and revealed what she was hiding. It was a pair of scissors.

"You know," Frida said, "we all feel really bad that we didn't get time to fix your hair before the prom." She turned the scissors over in her hands a couple of times. "So we thought we would help you out now." She squeezed the scissors and pretended to cut the air. "After all, I never got to truly thank you for helping me out with my hair that time."

I turned around and started to run.

"Get her!" Frida shouted.

Julie and Norunn caught up with me fast and grabbed my arms, holding me in a tight grip so that I couldn't go anywhere.

Frida moved the scissors closer to my face. I tried to wiggle and shake my head but there was nothing I could do. I heard the sound of the blades in my ear and I felt my brown curls falling down on my shoulders and then onto my feet. I didn't notice that I had started crying until my tears made it down to my lips and I tasted the salty drops.

"And now the other side," Frida said and moved the scissors around my head.

That was when I managed to wiggle out of their grip and I started to run away again. I managed to get all the way to the end of the pine trees without them catching me and I thought that I might be able to outrun them. I took random turns to the left and right, hoping they wouldn't work out which way I went.

Suddenly I heard someone behind me. They were close. It was hard to see where I was going as I was running further away from the lit path. Then I stepped on my dress and I tripped and fell over. As I tried to get up, someone pushed me down and I fell and ended up on my back. It was Frida. She climbed on top of my stomach and shouted, "I got her! Hurry up!"

Just as she lowered the scissors towards my head again I grabbed her hand. She kept trying to move them closer to me, but this time I was stronger.

"Let go!" she yelled.

I heard the girls running somewhere nearby. "Where are you?" one of them yelled.

I gathered all the strength that I had left to push the scissors away from me. I guess Frida wasn't expecting it, because all of a sudden they flew full force towards her and hit her in the face.

She screamed and fell back and I jumped to my feet. I looked at Frida. She was covering her right eye with her hand and blood was streaming down her face. And she was screaming.

Suddenly someone pushed me so I lost my balance. As I fell down I could see Julie in the corner of my eye. I landed on my right side and hit the ground really hard.

Then I heard something in my shoulder pop.

# Epilogue

It has been three months, two days and nineteen minutes since my last entry.

I will try and pick up from where I left off.

After the incident Frida had to have two stitches in her right eyebrow. They cleaned the blood and patched her up really quickly. She was told she most probably wouldn't even have a scar.

I had to go to the emergency room too. Since I was wearing a strappy dress it was easy to pull my shoulder back into place without too much fuss. I didn't need to get undressed or anything.

As the nurse put the sling around my shoulder she looked at me and said, "What happened?"

"I dislocated my shoulder."

"I mean to your hair."

I lifted my left hand up and felt my curls. On one side of my head they didn't even reach down to my chin. I hadn't seen myself in the mirror yet and I didn't know what it looked like. But I didn't need to see myself to know that I looked weird.

"Payback," I said.

When we got home that night my dad asked me what the hell was wrong with teenage girls these days. "It is like you can't be left alone without running around cutting each other's hair."

He said that it was not like this when he was growing up.

The day after he called my mom to let her know what happened and I was allowed to talk to her too. She said that everything would be fine and that I shouldn't worry. She also said that she was feeling a lot better and that she would be home soon. Soon meant twenty days, one hour and nineteen minutes.

A couple of days later, I had a visit from child protection services. They don't wait for you to respond to a letter. They just show up on your doorstep.

Unannounced.

I guess me opening the door with my arm in a sling and one side of my hair much shorter than the other wasn't the best first impression.

The lady was wearing a grey skirt suit, had short brown hair and tiny round glasses resting on a pointy nose. She looked like a character from *Postman Pat*.

She introduced herself and asked to come in, but it wasn't really a question, because she asked as she walked into my house. And she didn't take her shoes off.

Her name was Inger Larsen.

Inger asked where my mom was.

"Away," my dad said.

"She is not in prison," I said.

Then she insisted on talking to me alone and she asked me a lot of questions. First she asked me about why my arm was in a sling and I told her what happened.

I guess this time there was never really a fear that Frida would report me to the police.

Everyone – my mom, my dad, Sigve and now Inger – said that Frida was the one who tricked me into coming to the woods that night.

She was the one who attacked me.

She was the one trying to use the scissors on me.

I was acting in self-defence.

In fact, Inger asked if we were planning on reporting Frida to the police. I didn't want that though. I didn't want Frida as a friend, but I didn't want her as an enemy either. I just wanted to put the whole thing behind me.

Then Inger asked me questions about school and about my mom and dad. "Just to get a general overview of the situation," she said.

I am not sure if it was my school who contacted child protection services or if it was someone in the emergency room, but I heard that Frida had also had a visit from them.

After she was done asking me questions, she talked to my dad. I don't know exactly what they talked about, but he can't have told her too much. He normally doesn't talk about things.

There were a couple more follow-up meetings before it was decided that, in light of everything, it would be good for me to talk to a professional. That meant a psychiatrist.

My dad never wanted us to talk about our business to anyone, which was why he ignored that letter from CAPS. He didn't want people in Haasund to gossip about us. My mom said that this was because he had so much pride. Sigve said that he was just embarrassed.

Embarrassed that his daughter needed therapy. Embarrassed that his wife had a drinking problem. It was Sigve who told me that mom was in rehab. At first I thought he was messing with me, but I asked my mom about it the next time she called and she confirmed. She said she had had enough of all the lies and that we would talk more when she got home.

My first session with the therapist was meant to be on a Wednesday at 11 a.m., but it didn't start until 11.08. I sat in the waiting room and watched the minutes go by on the clock on the wall. The walls had different paintings of flowers on them, and in the corner of the room there was a tank with a lot of colourful fish. No matter how much they swam they didn't get anywhere. I lifted my hand and felt my much shorter hair. My head felt so much lighter now and I hadn't got used to it yet.

Aunt Lillian had given me a new hairdo. She said that I could still go to the hairdresser if I wanted, but she felt strongly that my hair at least needed to be the same length before walking into a salon. My curls are still all over the place and I don't look better with short hair the way Frida did. But my hair wasn't that good to begin with. Well, I guess that might depend on what sort of hair you like.

At 11.08 the therapist came out of her office. She had short blonde hair and wore a blue trouser suit. She held out her right hand to introduce herself, but my right arm was in a sling so I held out my left hand instead.

"Oh, sorry," she said and switched hands. "I'm Dagny."

I shook her hand. "Malin," I said.

She told me to please come into her office, which I did.

The room contained a few bookshelves and a hardwood desk that looked very neat. Apart from a computer there was nothing on the desk. She had a couple of diplomas on the wall and a painting of a house and some trees. There was also a black and gold clock, which had roman numerals on it. In the other half of the room were two chairs and, between them, a coffee table. Dagny held out her arm towards the chairs. "Have a seat," she said.

"Which chair?" I said.

"Whichever you want," she said.

I chose the one facing the wall because then I could see the clock.

Dagny sat down in the other chair and said, "How are you today?"

"I'm okay."

"What brings you here?"

"Child protection services told me I should talk to a professional."

"Why do you think they wanted you to do that?"

"I think because I was jumped by those girls in the woods, as that can be a traumatic experience. And because I had attacked Frida with a pair of scissors on a different occasion. And also, maybe, because my mom went away."

"Do you want to tell me what happened in the woods?"

And I did.

"How do you feel now?"

"I am having trouble sleeping."

"Why do you think that is?"

"I keep thinking about Frida."

The image of me accidentally stabbing Frida with the scissors kept appearing in my mind. When I closed my eyes I could see the blood running down her face and staining her dress.

"If the scissors had hit Frida half a centimetre lower I would have pierced her eye. She could have gone blind."

"But you didn't pierce her eye," Dagny said. "She didn't go blind."

Dagny taught me that there is no use thinking about everything that could have gone differently. Good or bad. You can drive yourself crazy imagining all the different scenarios that could possibly have taken place if you or someone else had made a different choice.

"What if Magnus hadn't taken his bike out that day? What if I didn't cut Frida's hair? What if my mom never started drinking?"

Dagny said that this kind of thinking is not fruitful, because you can't do anything to change the past. All you can do is change the future.

"Is there anything else you want to talk about?" Dagny said.

"Like what?"

She shrugged. "I don't know, like Magnus?"

When my mom came home from Oslo we had a long talk. She explained that her stay at the clinic had made her realize that she didn't actually need alcohol and that she now had a much more positive view on life. She also said that even though she felt perfectly fine towards the end of her stay and did not feel any urge to drink ever again, the day that it was time to leave the clinic she was absolutely petrified. But then, when she did go home, she felt okay. Better than she had felt in years. She was also the one who told me the truth about my cousin. Or, well, my brother.

What happened was this: about seventeen years ago things were not going so well between my mom and dad. They were struggling with money and it was hard to take care of a toddler and make ends meet and they were arguing a lot. My mom ended up having a short affair with another man and my dad moved out of the house for a bit. Around the same time Aunt Lillian was coming out of a bad break-up so they sought comfort in each other. And apparently the way to do that was to sleep together. By the time Aunt Lillian found out that she was pregnant my dad had already moved back in with my mom. At that point it wasn't really possible for anyone to do the right thing because they had all screwed up.

I didn't know what to say to it all, because it was a lot to take in and my head was spinning.

Magnus once told me that I was like a sister to him, but I didn't agree. I liked that he was my cousin because brothers and sisters don't get along. Turns out he was my brother after all. Well, I suppose he was both.

When I finally got my watch back, the stopwatch had been reset. It showed the time as 00.05.

At first this made me really sad, because it seemed so important to keep his record.

"Why do you think that is?" Dagny said.

"I don't know."

It was a bit hard to explain, because at first I hadn't even realized that the record was still in my watch. And then, once I found out, it was like realizing that a piece of him was still with me, which I guess seems a bit silly.

Dagny said she could relate to the loss I felt, because she once went to Paris on holiday and she lost her camera and all her pictures. At first she was upset, but then she realized that even though the pictures were gone, she still had her memories. I have never been to Paris, but I knew what she meant. Even though the record is no longer stored in my watch, I still remember it and no one can take that away from me.

I had my confirmation in May. I don't know how it is where you are from, but in Haasund almost everyone does this even if they are not religious at all. I heard that a lot of the kids in my class got more than 25000 kroner in gifts. I didn't get nearly as much, but I got something better. A white and silver Casio G-Shock digital watch. It is shock resistant and has five different alarms and an automatic LED light. It also has 200-metre water resistance. That means that I don't have to take it off when I go swimming. Unless I want to. Getting me a new watch was actually Sigve's idea. He even helped pick it out. If Magnus was still around he would have been the first person I would have shown it to. I think he would have really liked it.

Oscar had a check-up at the vet's. The doctor diagnosed him with feline obesity which is just a fancy word for a really fat cat. He said it was very important that Oscar lost weight because being overly obese will reduce a cat's quality of life and it can lead to more serious illnesses like diabetes or dysplasia and cause him to die at an early age. Hearing this made me feel really bad about all the treats I had been sneaking him, because I would never purposely do anything to harm him, and I really didn't want him to die.

So Oscar is back to eating dry cat food. Once a week he is allowed to have a bit of canned tuna, but no more bacon. Turns out a little fat can be harmful after all. At least if you are a cat.

Me and Ruben also had a chance to talk. I finally sent him a letter explaining everything and he came to my house.

"I never asked you to come to the woods," Ruben said. "That wasn't me."

"I know," I said. "And I never said you were gross."

"Okay."

It turned out that Ruben never even supported Frida's prom campaign. It was just another trick.

Ruben was very upset when he thought that I said those things about him. I was upset with him too, because he didn't give me a chance to explain. And I was disappointed that he would believe Frida over me. But

Frida can be very persuasive and she is hard to read. I, of all people, know that.

I don't think that everything between me and Ruben is broken. In fact, I am going over to his house to play video games this Saturday. And I have bought a pack of breath mints, just in case. It doesn't hurt to be prepared.


It has been four months, three days and eleven minutes since my last entry.

A lot has happened since then.

I am older and more mature. My breasts are larger too. Of course, I am fifteen now.

I am doing my third and final year of lower secondary school at a new place. In Bryne. That means that I have to cycle to the next village, and take the train from Nærbø at 7.30 a.m. every morning, Monday to Friday. Dagny felt that it would be good for me to get a fresh start somewhere else.

Bryne Lower Secondary School has a cafeteria where they have a selection of different sandwiches, plus yoghurts, milk and juice. And Monday, Wednesday and Fridays they have a warm meal. My mom let me get a punch card so that I can purchase food at school every day.

The kids at this school hang out in groups too. The boys

who play basketball are in one group and the girls who wear designer shoes are in another. I don't have a group. At least not yet. Making friends is not easy. Especially not at a new school.

My new maths teacher is named Frank Olsen. He often makes poor jokes and he smells like coffee, but apart from that he is okay. One day he held me back after class, because he wanted to talk to me. I wasn't in trouble. He said that he had noticed that my skill level was way above what was expected in his class. And after he discussed it with the school and my parents, it was decided that I should take an advanced maths class.

"You are really smart, Malin," Frank said.

No one had ever said that to me before.

I wasn't exactly sure where the room for advanced maths was, so for my first class I went early to make sure I had time to find it. When I got there a girl was sitting on the floor outside the room. She was reading a book called *Fun Facts*.

"Hello," I said.

The girl looked up from her book. "Oh, hi," she said. "Are you in the advanced maths class too?"

I nodded.

"I'm Oda," she said.

"Malin."

"Do you want to hear a fun fact?"

"Okay."

"Turns out Alexander Graham Bell didn't invent the phone after all."

"I know. It was Antonio Meucci."

"That's right. How did you know that?"

"I read a lot."

Oda smiled. "So do I."

I think I will be okay in this place. I only have one more year of lower secondary school anyway. And next year I can go wherever I want.

I have started going to physiotherapy twice a week. Most of the time I pull bands and lift dumb-bells. It is very boring, but sometimes you have to do something you don't like to improve your future. That is what my mom said anyway. After the sessions I normally go to Ruben's house, which means that I also have something to look forward to those days. Sometimes we play video games and sometimes we kiss, but mostly we just talk. I think it is important that we get to know each other properly. My mom said that is how you build trust.

I haven't seen much of Frida lately, so I can't tell you what she is up to.

I sent her a text a few months back and said that I was sorry that things turned out the way that they did, but she didn't reply. It is okay though, I have forgiven her, and maybe in time she will forgive me too.

After my parents told me everything I needed to know about Magnus, my dad went away for a couple of days.

"Is he going on a business trip?" I said.

"That's not funny," my mom said.

She said that he needed some time to himself. She also said he felt guilty and that he was worried that I hated him. And I did. I hated them both. Just a little. But they are my parents and I can't help but love them at the same time. Then my mom told me that she hadn't been a good mother to me lately. Actually, she wasn't sure if she had ever been a good mother to me, but she would like to get another chance. And even though bad things happened it was her own choice to drink.

I think she is doing okay. At least she doesn't forget things like she used to. And she makes dinner on time every day.

Aunt Lillian came to see me. I was sitting at the kitchen table reading my encyclopedia when she walked in carrying a brown paper bag.

"How are you, Malin?" she said.

"I'm fine."

"I was wondering if you could help me with something." She opened the bag and took out a shiny cup. I recognized it from Magnus's room. It was one of his swimming trophies.

"I was thinking of getting it engraved. Maybe you could help me decide what it should say. You knew him better than anyone."

I didn't answer right away so she took out her phone. "I've found some suggestions online; *Always in our hearts. Gone, but not forgotten.*"

I shook my head. "I know what it needs to say."

A few days later my dad came home.

"Hello, Malin," he said.

"Hello," I said.

Then Sigve and Katrine walked in. For some reason no one said hi or anything. We all just stood and looked at each other. Then Sigve held up a deck of cards. "Anyone up for a game?"

I couldn't remember the last time my family played cards together. In fact, I wasn't even sure it had ever happened before.

Katrine taught us this game called Play or Pay. The aim of the game is to be the first one to get rid of all your cards. The first person plays any card they want, and the rest need to continue in the same suit and the numbers need to be in a sequence. So if the first person plays a king of hearts, the next card needs to be an ace of hearts, then the two of hearts and so on. You cannot start a new suit until one is completed. If you can't play, you need to pay.

We used jelly beans as stakes and for some reason I kept winning. Twice in a row, I was the first one to get rid of all my cards and I had a huge pile of jelly beans in front of me.

"Wow, you are really good at this," Katrine said.

"She is probably counting cards or something," Sigve said. "I mean, isn't that the kind of thing that weirdos like her would do?"

Katrine smacked him in the shoulder and gave him an annoyed look.

"Malin is not a weirdo," my mom said.

My dad said, "Let's just play the game."

It is not even possible to count cards in that particular game. And you can't actually be good or bad at it. It all depends on luck and which cards you are dealt, but I decided not to mention that.

Then I started losing. We played two more rounds and by then I had lost all my jelly beans to Sigve. After our last game, Sigve and Katrine said they had to go because they were going to the cinema.

"Don't forget your jelly beans," I said.

Sigve shrugged. "Keep them."

Sigve still works at the shop and my dad feels strongly that he is making the wrong choice by not going back to school. But even though he doesn't like it, he doesn't yell as much as he did before. My mom says that Sigve needs to find his own way and if it is a mistake it is his mistake to make. Sigve is very happy with Katrine and we hardly ever see him any more. He is either at work or with her. When I, on a rare occasion, do see him, he seems a lot less angry than before and he doesn't make a fuss if he notices that I have used his Xbox or touched his stuff.

He brought Katrine over for dinner one day. He said that in a year's time, when Katrine finishes upper secondary school, they are going to get an apartment together. My dad scoffed and my mom smiled. And we didn't talk about it any more.

So not everything has changed.

After Katrine left, my dad took Sigve aside. "Just make sure she doesn't get pregnant," he said.

Sigve said, "I will even make sure that her sister doesn't get pregnant."

\* \* \*

Hanna had her baby. I met her the other day when she was out walking with the stroller. She didn't show me the middle finger this time. Instead she stopped and said hi. The baby was very tiny. I didn't know that humans could be that small.

"Her name is Sofie," Hanna said.

"Did you and Patrik get an apartment?"

"No…" She paused for a minute. "We broke up actually. I mean, he has a lot on his mind these days, with getting his trade certificate and all. We will get back together when things calm down. Probably."

I nodded. "So where do you live?"

"With my mom."

Hanna explained that when she told her mom she wasn't going through with the abortion they had a huge argument. But as soon as little Sofie had been born, Hanna's mom had instantly fallen in love with the little girl and now she enjoyed being a grandma more than anything.

"I'm sorry," I said. "About what I called you that time. You are not a whore."

"I know," Hanna said.

After that, we didn't seem to have much more to say to each other. So we smiled and said goodbye and walked in separate directions.

I don't think I will be seeing much of Hanna in the future. We didn't say anything, but I think we both knew it.

Sigve created a Tinder account for Aunt Lillian. He said that it was time for her to meet a real man. Aunt Lillian laughed and said that that was not for her.

"At least that is what I thought at first," she said later. "But before I knew it I found myself swiping left and right." Whatever that means. Then she asked Sigve if he could help her increase the radius on the app, because with the current settings it only allowed her to meet local guys. "If there were any good men in Haasund, I would know about it," she said. She still doesn't know if Tinder is the way to go, but at least it is a start. "A start of something new."

My mom found out about the broken giraffe. She was dusting the shelf and noticed the cracked figurine I had tried to hide.

She picked it up and said, "What happened?"

I looked at the floor. "It was an accident," I whispered.

"I see."

"Maybe I can save up and buy a new one?"

My mom shrugged. "I think it is fine the way it is." She quickly dusted the giraffe off and put it back on the shelf next to the others.

She said that not everything in life can be fixed. Sometimes you just have to find a way to live with what is broken and move on.

I looked at the giraffe. The lump of glue around its neck really made it stand out from the rest of the collection. I decided I liked it better this way. It wasn't perfect, but it was different. And that made it special.

I kept trying to avoid talking about Magnus in therapy, but Dagny kept returning to the subject. Apparently it was very important that we talked about it. Dagny can be very persuasive. And before I knew it, I willingly told her all about him. And it felt good.

Throughout my life, Magnus had been the only person who was always there for me, no matter what. And he accepted me as I was, no matter what I said or how I acted.

Then I started crying. I never told Magnus how much I loved him, and now I never could.

Dagny said, "Do you wish you knew that he was your brother earlier?"

I shook my head. "No."

"Why not?"

"Magnus was a great cousin. If he knew he was my brother, he would probably have hated me."

"You think so?"

I nodded. "Cousins are better."

The sun was peeking through the clouds as we crossed the graveyard. My mom and Aunt Lillian were both carrying flowers and as they were walking they talked about the weather and the news. And other ordinary things. Sigve walked a few metres behind everyone else, checking his phone. My dad took huge steps as we walked through the wet grass and I clutched the trophy to my chest as I struggled to keep up with him.

We turned left at a lamp post and Aunt Lillian led the way past the graves. Some of them were nearly overgrown with tall grass, while others had fresh flowers and some even had toys and teddy bears.

Magnus's grave was really well kept and had nice flowers and a lantern. That made sense because Aunt Lillian tends to it at least once a week. For the rest of us it was the first time we had been to visit and that made me feel bad. But at least we were there now. And you can't do anything to change the past. All you can do is change the future.

The headstone was in dark granite and shaped like a heart. It said,

*In loving memory of*
*Magnus Helvik*
*You left us way too soon*


"It's a beautiful stone," my mom said.

Then they put down the flowers and Aunt Lillian lit the candle in the lantern.

I looked up at my dad and for a moment I thought I saw a tear in the corner of his eye. But then he blinked and it was gone and I might have just imagined it.

I pictured Magnus looking down at us and thinking about what a complete mess his family was. But he had forgiven everyone because in heaven everything is perfect and there is no pain. At least that's how I imagine it.

Before Magnus died I wasn't sure if I believed in heaven, but the thought of him just lying in the ground and being nowhere was too hard.

I caught Sigve's eye and I was waiting to see if he would tell me that I was being silly and that this whole thing was stupid, but instead he nodded and gave me a half smile.

So I took a step forward and whispered, "I love you, Magnus." Then I put the trophy down and turned it around so the inscription became visible.

It said, *00:04:46 – Personal Best.*

If I got to be God for one day I would make sure that everyone gets a second chance. Because everyone screws up sometimes. One way or another.

My dad definitely took some wrong turns in his life, Like the time he cheated on my mom with Aunt Lillian. When my mom found out about the pregnancy she felt lost and hurt and didn't know where to turn or where to go. So she stayed with my dad and agreed it was best to keep it a secret. But watching Magnus grow up with Aunt Lillian's smile and my dad's eyes made her resent him and love him all at the same time. So she turned to alcohol to ease the pain a little. Wine made things better in the short run but it made everything a lot worse in the long run. I don't really know what that means, but that is what she said. She also said that this was just a trigger, and that it was nobody's fault but her own that she started drinking. "You know," she said. "One way or another I would have become an alcoholic. It was just on the cards for me."

I remember that time I asked Magnus about his dad. When I mentioned that my dad wasn't great either he said, "At least you got one." And he was right.

My dad has not always been the best dad to me and Sigve, but he sure was a lousy dad to Magnus. The fact that he never gets to repair this or make things right with

Magnus is his punishment. He doesn't need me or anyone else to punish him further.

I messed up too. Especially when it came to my friendship with Hanna. Hanna was nice to me and she did stick up for me, but we are very different. My mom said it is because of our age difference and that no sixteen year old should be friends with a fourteen year old.

"Magnus was my friend and he was nearly seventeen," I said.

"That is different," my mom said. "Magnus was your cousin."

"And brother," I said.

Whatever the differences between me and Hanna were, it did not give me the right to call her a whore. I don't think it is ever okay to call someone a whore.

Despite everything that happened, I wouldn't take any of it back. Not even that time when I cut Frida's hair.

Not because I think that everything that happened was good, but I don't think you can just choose to change certain things in your life that didn't turn out exactly the way you wanted. I don't think it works that way. I think that's cheating.

I would just make it so that everyone gets a fresh start and a chance to make things right again. Just like me and my family are working on right now.

If I got to be God for one day I would probably not be able to fix everything that is wrong in this world. But I would like to try and make sure that everyone feels at least okay once in a while. Because sometimes okay is enough.

# Author's Note

I think I was around nine years old the first time I said that I was going to be an author – and I said it with the utmost confidence. Because back then writing was so easy. Obviously not because I was better at it, but because I never questioned myself. I just trusted that everything I wrote was a true masterpiece.

One of my first stories was about a mouse named Robinson who was looking for his hat. He found it halfway through and then the story ended up being about him trying to get a hold of some cheese without being caught by Lurifaks, the cat. Plot twist! It didn't make much sense, but to me that didn't matter. Because I didn't know.

I remember very clearly when I first started writing, but I don't remember when I stopped.

I might have been around sixteen when it started to play less and less of a part in my life. None of my friends were into writing, it seemed like a strange hobby to have and I guess I just got busy doing things that seemed more important at the time.

To me it doesn't really matter why I spent so many years of my life not writing. The most important thing is that I found my way back to it.

When I started my MA course I was very surprised when I ended up writing stories that took place in small Norwegian towns. After all, this was an environment that I had felt I so desperately needed to escape.

I think there has always been a small part of me that felt like I didn't belong in my home town. That I was different from everyone else. And didn't fit in. And I am pretty sure people thought I was different too. The thing about small towns is that it doesn't necessarily take much for you to stand out, and if you stand out in any way, chances are you are a weirdo.

There was also a part of me that loved my home town. I had the best of friends and being part of a community where everyone knew each other and felt comfortable and safe. At one point I was 100% sure I would stay there for ever.

I dreamed of me and my mates getting flats in the same building and that we would hang out all the time and visit each other on a daily basis just like one long episode of *Friends*.

But like most things in my life this feeling didn't last too long. Around age twenty one I remember being very restless and bored and I had no clue what I wanted to do in the future.

I strongly felt the need to go as far away as humanly possible. So I went to Australia.

Four months before my visa expired I had run out of money and I couldn't afford my return ticket, so I worked as a dishwasher every day for two months to earn enough money to go back to Norway. I honestly thought that this journey would solve everything. That I would find myself and suddenly all the answers as to what I should do with my life.

Today I am just as restless and I constantly have the need to go somewhere else and experience something new. The way I see it, I don't have a home. When I go back to my home town I am just visiting a place where I used to live. Every time I move somewhere it feels like a place where I live for the time being, because I know I won't be there for long.

I used to think that one day in the future I would be able to settle down, but now I am not so sure. And maybe this is the reason I am fascinated by the place I grew up. The people who live there seem so content and happy. And at peace. But I know that this place isn't right for me any more and everyone needs to find their own version of happiness.

*The Unpredictability of Being Human* started with me burning a bag of popcorn. I knew nothing about the character or the story when I wrote the first couple of lines and I really did not expect it to end up being a novel. The first chapter was originally a short story and I thought that I was done. But then I realized that there was so much more to explore about this character and I really enjoyed writing in her voice so I decided to see where I could take it.

The characters and Malin's personality all came rather spontaneously. It was a strange way to write because normally I would at least have some sort of an idea of a story, a scene or a character before starting. But it was a very interesting process and I loved getting to know Malin as I wrote it.

Today, writing is not fun and easy all the time. It is hard and frustrating and I often find myself staring at a blank page, scared to get started. Because getting started is often the toughest part. The true magic for me is the moments where everything starts to come together. I love re-writing and editing myself and making it better. And then I'm reminded why I love writing so much. It is kind of like the relief you feel after finishing an exam.

Or when you dislocate your shoulder, and they pop it back in and the pain eases up and makes you feel that it was all worth it. (Well, not really.)

I have becomes a true master at procrastination. While writing this author's note I have watched numerous YouTube videos, found out which Disney Prince is my soulmate and what I should name my cat (I don't even have a cat).

But as long as you get there in the end it is okay. And sometimes okay is enough.

For the past three years I have been a part time cartoonist who can't draw.

And now I am a writer. Who can't spell.

# About
# Linni Ingemundsen

Linni Ingemundsen is from Norway, though she currently lives in Malta. She does not know how to draw but is somehow a freelance cartoonist. Some of her favourite things in life include chocolate, free Wi-Fi and her yellow typewriter.

Linni has lived in three different countries and will never be done exploring the world. She has worked as a dishwasher in Australia, a volunteer journalist in Tanzania and has approximately 2.5 near-death experiences behind her. Still, what truly inspires her writing is her background growing up in a village on the south-western coast of Norway.

Linni began writing *The Unpredictability of Being Human* while on the Oxford Brookes MA in Creative Writing. Her dark, comical storytelling introduces her readers to a small-town community filled with pain, humour and a whole lot of nothingness.

# Unpredictable Book Club Questions

- If you were God for a day, what would you change and what would you leave as it is? Why?

- The book is set in a small town in Norway. Discuss the location and its role in the book.

- Look at the ways the teenage characters in the book – Malin, Sigve, Magnus, Hanna and Frida – interact with their parents, and consider the similarities and differences. How are families depicted in the book more generally?

- Were you surprised when you discovered the identity of Magnus's father? Do you think Magnus knew who his father was? Does it matter to you if he did? Does it change your reading of events in the book?

- Discuss the role of time, both in the book, and in Malin's life.

- On p67, Ruben begins to ask Malin a question, but does not finish it. What did you think he was going to ask her?

- What was your opinion of Frida at the beginning of the book? Did this change while you were reading? How did you feel about her by the end?

- The alligator snapping turtle, a giraffe, snakes and elephants all make an appearance in the book. What significance might these moments have?

- If you knew Malin, do you think you would be friends with her? Whatever your answer, explore your reasons.

- How did reading this book make you feel? Did you laugh? Did you cry? Did any of your responses surprise you?

- The book is called *The Unpredictability of Being Human*. What does this title mean to you? What does it mean to be human?

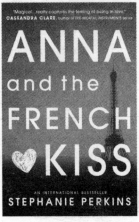